FLYING V

RISHABH PURI is an ...
business in Nigeria, Dub... ...emanding
day job, he finds time to indulge in his passion for writing fiction,
and his first book, *Inside the Heart of Hope* was published in 2017.
Diagnosed with a life-threatening heart disease at the age of 1,
Rishabh's early life was mostly limited to talking to doctors and
visiting hospitals for several major surgeries and regular check-
ups. Now, armed with the resilience and experience his fierce
battles with the disease brought him, Rishabh has taught himself
to live life to the fullest against all odds. His writings too, are
mostly centered on the beauty of hope, love and life.

Rishabh is also an avid traveller and a supercar enthusiast. He
is based in Lagos, Nigeria but visits India regularly, returning to
his birthplace, Chandigarh, which remains immensely close to his
heart.

Follow Rishabh online on:
Facebook : AuthorRishabhPuri
Twitter : @AuthorRPuri
Instagram : @officialrishabhpuri

RAVINDER SINGH

PRESENTS

FLYING
WITHOUT
WINGS

RISHABH PURI

HarperCollins *Publishers* India

Black Ink

HarperCollins Publishers
Since 1817

First published in India by
HarperCollins *Publishers* India and Black Ink in 2017
A-75, Sector 57, Noida, Uttar Pradesh 201301, India
www.harpercollins.co.in

2 4 6 8 10 9 7 5 3 1

Copyright © Rishabh Puri 2017

P-ISBN: 978-93-5277-320-6
E-ISBN: 978-93-5277-321-3

Typeset in 11/13.7 Arno Pro at
Manipal Digital Systems, Manipal

Printed and bound at
Thomson Press (India) Ltd.

PREFACE

Every new day is a miracle. There is a chance for your fortunes to change, blessings to fall upon you like rain. You may see a new mercy, sing a new song, or feel joy like you've never felt before. I am thankful that today, you've picked up my novel and decided to read it.

Not every day of my life has been blessed with good health and fortune. In fact, many of my days have been filled with suffering and loneliness. From my diagnosis with a rare disease while I was still in infancy, to the surgeries I've had to undergo as a result and the sleepless nights filled with gruelling pain I've had to suffer, through, I have had some bad luck in my life.

But out of it has come the ability to write truth, a deeper appreciation for the life I live, and above all, an overwhelming gratitude for the people with whom I share this life. I believe that writing this book presents me with an opportunity to thank them publicly, and I'd like to gratefully take it.

First and foremost, I would like to thank God for the profuse blessings that he has showered upon me and the joy I've experienced in this life. I would also like to thank my parents and my sister for their unstinting love and support all through my life. Not everyone is as graced as I am with a family who loves and cares for me the way you do. Without you I would be lost.

I would like to thank my doctors who have stood by my side and taken incredible risks to give me a full, healthy life, and find me a reprieve from my pain. Dr Dennis Lox, thank you for your expertise and the countless hours you've devoted to my case. Also, thank you for making me laugh on some of the darkest days of my life. Your care for me has strengthened me beyond belief. To Dr Saminathan Suresh Nathan, my gratitude for the years of study and expertise you have attained which lead me to you, is beyond what words can communicate. Your work has changed my life for better. I am beyond grateful.

And finally, I would like to thank you, dear reader, for opening this book. It is not every day that gives birth to a project of passion. It is not every day that a man can wake up to see one of his dreams realized for all to behold and enjoy. What you are reading today is a product of my passion, one of my dreams brought to life. So today is an incredible day. Thank you for reading. I hope you enjoy this book.

PROLOGUE

The night Karan first installed Clikrr on his phone was the loneliest of his life. That night he lay in his bed next to yet another woman who didn't love him. Their bodies turned away from each other, as if trying to escape the other's touch unconsciously. Their breaths felt out of sync. She slept peacefully enough beside him, dreaming, no doubt, of the life of luxury Karan's wallet would provide. Trips to Mykonos and fine perfumes, Birkin bags and Louboutins. She slept deeply on silk sheets, completely oblivious to the man in turmoil beside her.

Karan lay awake, tossing and turning. The dim moonlight through the window seemed too bright for him to handle. The dark shadows in the room too heavy around him, pressing down hard against his chest. He felt suffocated by the oppressive scent of the girl's perfume embedded in his bed sheets. The mansion where he grew up, which had once been his haven, became his prison. And he, his own gaoler.

Why did he do this to himself? He had sought to escape from his pain in luxury: in fast cars, in good wine, in fine dining and in finer women. He had earned the best that money could buy, the way his father had before him. However, it now tasted like ashes in his mouth.. He had one of the most beautiful women in the world on his arm, the kind of woman who turned heads everywhere she went, but her heart wasn't turned towards him.

He had built himself a palace of little substance with barely any sentiments. If the place burned to the ground, he would hardly have lost anything at all.

He couldn't find women to love him in luxury yacht clubs, in Ferrari dealerships and in members-only airport lounges. Those women only loved luxury, and had no room in their hearts for true love. Perhaps they too sought to fill their empty hearts the same way he did. In any case, as long as they were buried together in these trappings of useless extravagance, and vapid time-wasting and boring vacations month after month, could they ever truly see each other?

No, he thought, they couldn't.

He keyed in the initiating pattern on his phone and got ready to download Clikrr. He had debated doing this for weeks, but his loneliness hadn't hurt so sharply until this moment. What else could he do to relieve the pain? He scrolled through the app's features, reading the reviews and generally stalling. If he was honest with himself, the truth would be that he was scared. Love frightened him. It intrigued him, fascinated him, and most of his life had been spent chasing it. But the thought of actually catching it, of having to bare all and put it on the line for one woman … it made him go cold. Uncomfortable. Afraid.

Of course, all the women he had ever met seemed the type to destroy him. If he were brave or foolish enough to bare his soul to them, they would tear him apart looking for treasure. If he could find the one woman who he could trust with his innermost workings, his secret fears, the story of his life in all its tragedies and complexities, perhaps then he could let go.

However, the moment he started to like someone, it was invariably the same old story. He was quick to erect battlements around his heart. He wielded his every charm like a weapon, a glittering smile like a Portcullis preventing her from getting inside his mind, or worse, breaking his heart. When his heart started to flutter with thoughts of infatuation and even love, he would remember the way the woman before had torn him down and his defences would come up, almost of their own volition. She would find him cold where he was once warm; cruel where he was once kind. Perhaps if he could let her in, it would be a different story. But, as it was, she grew cold in return. Manipulations and games began. Heartbreak followed.

His father ran the company's business ventures in Africa, while Karan managed the Indian branch of the company; dutiful and miserable. 'You need a wife,' his father had chided the last time they spoke on the phone, 'but you need to meet the right woman first.'

It was easier said than done. He had tried to convince himself at first that money was what made him happy and that he could survive on sex. Love hadn't seemed to be a possibility even back then. He numbed his fear of rejection with hook-ups, bad dates and worse ideas. But he hadn't been able to quell the terror in his heart or the longing voice that said, 'Maybe, coming home to someone instead of waking up alone would not be so bad.' But sometimes, love to Karan seemed like giving someone a handsaw or a titanium hammer with which to handle his heart, yet standing back and hoping they wouldn't use the tools he'd given them against him.

But Karan had seen the way his parents adored each other, the way they built a castle of their love and housed a family within it. Which was why, despite the failed relationships and hook-ups, despite all the women who had used him in some quest for money, glory, power, or something to fill the hole in their hearts, Karan still believed in love. He still craved for it.

He dreamed of her sometimes, whoever 'she' was. The one person who could conquer his heart and ignite his soul. He dreamed of the one woman who would open her arms to him and hold him tight, promising to never let go. He dreamed of a feeling that would last a lifetime, through good times and bad, a woman who really meant it when she said 'I love you' to him and not mean 'I love your fortune'.

She had to be somewhere, he knew. Waiting for him, dreaming of him too. Burying herself in books like him, reading stories of love to fill the void of having no one. Soon enough, he promised himself, they would have each other. They would hold each other forever in that perfect kiss. He just had to find her first.

So he opened up Clikrr and started to swipe, left and right through a myriad faces and interesting profiles, hoping someone would catch his eye. Perhaps they would come together magically, mutual love at first sight, the kind of love that healed all their hurts and swept away all their problems. The kind of love that replaced the need for food or air, the kind that made two people depend wholly on each other.

He couldn't bring himself to believe that love worked like that. Not with all the hurt that he had been through in this life. Nevertheless, as he swiped through profile after profile, wondering who might enchant him and who would irrevocably break his heart, he hoped that he would find the one person on earth who could prove him wrong.

ONE

Everything in Chandigarh International Airport existed in a state of flux. Everything that is, except Milli. Day after day, she observed the whirling mass of people moving through the liminal space of gates F8-F14 from her perch behind the counter of the duty-free shop. From her still spot behind the desk, seated, as it were, in the eye of the hurricane, she had an unimpeded view of the planes shuttling off people who were more exciting than she was to destinations that were more exciting than anything she had ever seen. In all her years of working at the airport, Milli had never seen the inside of a plane. But, with a view like the one from the airport window, she could definitely daydream.

It was a good view to have, the planes flying in and out of sight, returning from and heading towards fascinating foreign places. It was certainly better than the one her friends deployed elsewhere at the concourse had. Sometimes she looked up while helping a customer and glimpsed the sunset through the glass. Sometimes there were people worth watching: the beautiful, the glamorous, and the plain crazy. She was uncertain what exactly to make of the couple who had just come in lay, but she was willing to set her novel down for half a moment to find out.

The man was fit and tan, trim and tailored, manicured to a T with coiffed hair and the kind of smile that could only be achieved with thousands of rupees of dental work. If he was thirty, he had only just turned. He was model handsome, his eyes dark as a bitter sip of coffee, and as electrifying when they met hers. He was tall, but his open posture made him seem even taller, as though he was too used to the attention of the masses to wilt in its glare. A glint of gold at his wrist suggested a showy watch, the kind a man inherits from his father or was gifted as a bonus by his boss. It was clear that both him and the simpering woman on his arm were wealthy, and also clear that money had gone straight to their heads and affected them to their very core.

'Spoiled rotten' was the phrase that struck Milli's mind as she looked the woman over. Either she was younger than the man she was pouting at, with full, perfectly glossed lips, or her plastic surgeon was worth the massive investment she had no doubt made in him. She was the kind of woman who made Milli feel like a scenery, some blurred image in the background of the woman's high resolution life.

Milli had been called pretty many times before, but never beautiful. She had rivulets of raven-dark hair with a tendency to frizz in the simmering Chandigarh heat and guileless pondwater green eyes that held sorrow. The wear of hard work was evident on her calloused hands, and ever since her brother had been deployed, her muscles had grown toned from the manual labour it took to keep her ramshackle home from falling completely apart. She was curvy, although she never dressed to accentuate her body. If she had the money to spend on makeup and feminine frippery like the woman in front of her, she might have been able to lacquer herself into someone that could turn heads and make men fall in love. As it was, the drugstore makeup she could only afford made her look cheap, so she often went without any on at all.

When she looked at the mirror, Milli could sometimes see beauty in the softness of her features, the kindness that the world hadn't managed to wear away was evident on her face. But against this burnished beauty, someone who had nothing to do but look pretty, Milli felt plain indeed.

Milli had to tame the expression on her face to keep her lip from curling in distaste as the woman affected a baby voice. Milli had never begged for anything in her life, especially not in such an irritating manner.

'But honey,' the woman whined, peering pathetically at the man over the rim of her bug-eyed sunglasses, 'don't you think I deserve a present? I've been very, very good,' she added in a stage whisper that Milli could hear without straining to listen. She managed to restrain herself from rolling her eyes at the woman's display, but the man didn't bother trying to coach his expression of annoyance. He told the woman something that Milli couldn't catch, and she stalked off, apparently satisfied, to peruse bottles of expensive perfume.

The man sighed, shifting uncomfortably in a way that seemed out of character to Milli. It intrigued her. She had never seen a rich man break his poise in the way that this man was doing now. She studied his profile as he turned away, his dark eyes flitting over bottles of liquor. His lack of interest in it was nearly palpable. His hand reached absently to fiddle with the band of his watch, a little loose even on his thick wrist. Milli figured the band of his watch alone would sell for more than the pay cheque she would be taking home this month. Watching him carelessly click and unclick the clasp mechanism on the strap, she felt that he didn't really appreciate it monetary worth. Perhaps he didn't care.

Her phone began to vibrate beneath the counter where she had left it to charge. She barely needed to turn her gaze away from the man and towards her screen to know who was calling, Rahull again. He and her mother were the only people who didn't seem to understand that she couldn't answer her phone while on the clock. She pressed ignore on his call, considering, but ultimately dismissing, the thought of sending him a text with a reminder not to phone while she was working. She knew he would just ignore it and take the text as an invitation to further harass her.

Rahull was one of the people in her life who often called her pretty, and one of the reasons she had grown wary of the term. As a child, his affection towards her had been flattering, but as they grew, it became little more than a source of irritation and guilt for Milli. Rahull had fallen in love with her. And she hadn't fallen back. She had wanted to reciprocate his feelings for her – he was a hardworking man, a good provider who loved his family and would love her too. But she couldn't force her heart to want something it didn't. And it didn't want Rahull.

She looked up as a shadow fell across the counter. Standing in front of her was the man she had been observing, all tanned skin and electric eyes. Milli felt something within her stir, but she quickly tamped it down. He had selected a small bottle of scotch that Milli knew without having to refer was worth about as much as the expansive collection of quickly emptying bottles that her mother hid under the bed. He flashed her a winning smile, white as a bleached bone, as their eyes met.

He motioned to something behind her. 'Looks like we've got similar taste,' he said. Milli bit her lip to stop herself from saying that she seriously doubted they had anything in common. But he was digging in his carry-on for something and before she could respond, he had extracted a battered paperback out of his case. She was surprised to see that the cover was the same as the book she had been sneaking looks at during her downtime.

'I'm only three-quarters of the way through, so no spoilers,' he joked, fanning through the thin pages of the paperback to show her how much he had read. 'If I had any choice in the matter, I would have finished it in one read-through, but I've been a little … distracted,' he trailed off, throwing a look towards the woman who was currently sniffing samples of perfume like there were traces of cocaine on the thin strips of paper.

'Travelling will do that to you,' Milli offered with her best customer-service smile. The man shrugged, stowing the book back in his pack. He looked as though he was going to turn away. 'I'm only halfway through—' she offered quickly, before he could leave. She was uncertain as to why she wanted to hold his attention so badly. She was nothing like the vapid, beautiful women who clearly held him captive. She could never be a part of his world. 'But I only started reading it this morning.' His smile was softer this time, considering, approving. It made Milli feel warm.

'Smart girl,' he commented. 'You'll probably finish before I do.'

'I'll let you know how it ends,' she joked, drumming her fingers across the cover of the book nervously. Her phone began to buzz. 'Sorry, sorry—' she apologized, reaching down to ignore Rahull's call once again. 'I know I'm not supposed to have it on me at work.'

He waved his hand dismissively, 'You're not bothering me at all. Clingy boyfriend?'

'Nothing like that,' she muttered, putting her phone on silent. 'Just a kid from secondary school I haven't managed to shake yet.'

'It's a hard thing to do sometimes,' he allowed, as though he really did understand. 'Sometimes people become so much of a habit in your life that it doesn't matter whether you like them or not. Having them around is easier than being alone.'

It was only then that Milli realized that she recognized the awkwardness in his posture, the strange look in his eyes. The man in front of her was lonely, like her. She wondered how he could feel that way with his obvious affluence and his well-tailored clothes, and the dark-haired beauty on his arm. Certainly, they were nothing alike. But she was certain of what she saw in him: a lonely man lay hidden behind the gleaming smile.

She couldn't help but see him differently, as though she had recognized a kindred spirit in him from another life. She imagined the rainy streets of Paris, the glowing streetlamps illuminating their path as they ran hand in hand down the pavement, pausing under the awning of a rare and used bookstore for him to take her in his arms and press a kiss to her lips. The image took a moment to shake, and when she refocused, the man was still standing in front of her, amusement glinting in his dark eyes.

He took her hand in his and she tried to return his handshake with a firm grip.

'It's a pleasure to meet you,' he said, 'my name is—'

At that moment, the woman from before deposited a load of liquor and perfumes on the counter and draped herself around the man's arm with a dramatic sigh. 'Karan,' she trilled with a perfectly glossed smile, 'I'm done now.' She stuck out a hand, her manicured nails gleaming, painted a shade of red that Milli usually associated with warning signs.

The man – Karan – gave a one-armed shrug and an apologetic smile to Milli that seemed to suggest, 'Girlfriends: what can you do?' He fished his credit card from his wallet and handed it over to Milli. Satisfied that she had got what she wanted, the woman flounced off without so much as a 'thank you.' But it all barely registered to Milli. She swiped his card absently, her mind suddenly miles away. Her brother, also called Karan, was serving in Kashmir right now. How odd it was to run into a man with the same name, especially one who seemed so captivating to Milli. She pondered upon it as she packaged the gifts the man had purchased for his girlfriend.

'Well,' the man said, a little awkwardly, struggling only for a moment to lift the packages before he managed to balance them in a way that worked for him, 'enjoy your book.'

'You enjoy yours too,' Milli replied, unsure of what else to say. She felt a nearly crazy urge to ask him to stay and talk for a while, but he was already moving towards his gate. In no time at all, he would be whisked away on a jet, another fascinating person off to some fascinating place Milli would never be able to visit. She had to accept that fact and let him go.

So, she gave him a little wave and a smile, which he returned, all gleaming white teeth and dark, intelligent eyes. In another life, she thought to herself, they might have made it work. In another life, where Milli was fascinating, she would be at the gate next to him, both of them flipping through the same novel. But in this life he struggled under the weight of his girlfriend's presents and Milli turned back to her novel with a sigh. Her phone flashed a series of texts on its screen, this time from her mother.

MILLI PLS ANSWER MY CALL, it read.

MILLI BAJWA ANSWER ME NOW

ANSWER RAHULL'S CALL PLS

MILLI CALL ME ASAP. IT'S ABOUT KARAN

The sinking feeling in the pit of Milli's stomach which had started when the man walked away grew deeper, so heavy that Milli thought it might swallow her whole. With numb fingers, she misdialled her mother's number, then dialled again. This time the call went through. When her mother answered, all Milli could hear over the line was sobbing.

'Milli, it's Karan—' Her mother managed to get out, before breaking down once more. By the time Rahull took the phone from her mother, tears were already welling in Milli's eyes. She didn't need Rahull to voice what she already knew.

'An Improvised Explosive Device went off while he was on patrol,' Rahull said, his guttural voice even more hoarse with emotion. 'He didn't survive it. Milli, your brother is gone.'

Milli hung up without another word. She wasn't sure that she could even speak. Craning her neck, she searched in vain for the man who shared her brother's name, or the vapid beauty who clung to him. But they were nowhere to be found.

Despite the maelstrom of people churning around her, Milli felt utterly alone.

TWO

Two Months Later

The metallic clank of the gate opening rang in Milli's ears like an alarm clock, playing out like the opening notes to the song of her life. The counter smelled of pink disinfectant when she bent down to tuck her battered-looking purse into the cubby-hole behind it. The familiar scent was impersonal and sweet, cloying in her nose. The dull glint of the shiny pigment in the tile sparkled all the brighter as Harman, the sweet janitor assigned to the night shift at their gate drew her mop across its surface. The sun wouldn't rise for another half an hour at least, and the people who were gathered at the gates moved sluggishly like zombies in the dark. There wasn't enough coffee in the airport or force of will in their bodies to make them rush at this hour on the cusp of morning.

'Good morning, Milli!' Harman greeted her thickly, dipping her mop back into the bucket of grey water. Harman was always happy to see Milli, mainly because seeing Milli signified to her that her shift was nearly over. Milli liked Harman. She liked the strength in the determined set of the older woman's shoulders as she finished the last rounds of her shift, or the mothering tone she took with Milli as she tutted over her tired eyes. 'Show your teeth,' Harman teased now. 'It's not such a bad day as your scowl suggests, is it?'

Milli liked Harman enough that she wouldn't give her an honest answer to her question. How could it be a good day, when she was breathing but her brother was not? Nevertheless, she let her smile widen until it satisfied the other woman, showing a few white teeth until Harman howled with laughter. Milli unlocked the cash drawer and extracted the currency notes as Harman wrung out her mop. 'Good night?' she asked the other woman, who hummed to herself as she scrubbed a difficult spot on the floor.

'Some damn kid puked right outside the restrooms,' Harman shrugged. Milli winced sympathetically, expertly flipping through the bills. 'Apparently, the mom and dad thought he was faking when he told them he was feeling sick. By the time they figured out he wasn't, ka-blam! All over the carpet. But apart from that, can't complain.' Harman rarely complained, even when she could. It was a trait that Milli envied and wanted to emulate. 'Anu's coming in early, which means I can clock out a little early too. Wake my kids up before they head to school. It is a good day.'

Milli smiled and nodded, relocking the drawer and cracking her knuckles. She couldn't bring herself to agree with Harman, but she could at least play along. Milli saw no reason to bring Harman down with her personal problems on a day that was going so well for the other woman.

Harman gave a floor a once over, and then smiled with satisfaction. 'There, that's good enough for the richie riches coming in today, I think,' she said, teasing a smile back onto Milli's face. 'Anyway, they're not going to see how shiny the floor is when they've got a face that pretty behind the counter.'

'Harman!' Milli blushed, embarrassed.

'I just tell it like it is, girlie,' Harman let out a wicked cackle, backing her cart out of the duty-free. 'Charming kid like you, it's a wonder none of this new money has picked you up and put you with 'em on the next plane to whichever expensive and tropical place they're all going these days.'

'I've never been much for beaches,' Milli shrugged. 'More of a "books" kind of a girl.'

'Hey, someday your prince will come.' Harman winked, 'So don't bury your nose so far into one of those novels that you miss him when he does.'

'I swear that I won't,' Milli promised wryly, waving the novel in her hand at Harman. The other woman rolled her cart away with a laugh too strident for the early hour, leaving Milli alone with her thoughts and her book.

Very little happened during the morning that might have forced Milli to tuck her book away, so she read without interruption until well past the break of dawn. On the movie screen of her mind, the hero and heroine lay tangled in a sunset stained embrace, fearless of what the night might bring because they had each other. The language was overwrought, the plot a little unbelievable, but Milli still found herself mesmerized.

The screeching of rubber soles against tiles brought her out of her reverie, and she looked up, startled to find a boy, who couldn't have been much older than four, come sliding into the duty-free, knocking down a display of chocolates in his wake.

'Daksh! No! Daksh!' His mother was hot on his heels, biting down a swear as she took in the mess he had made. The boy was looking up wide-eyed at Milli from his position on the floor. She stared a moment longer back at him than she should have, trying to evaluate the extent of the damage. It looked like a small hurricane had whirled through the chocolates display. The situation was made all the worse when the boy burst into shocked tears.

'I'm so sorry!' the woman exclaimed, scooping the crying boy in one arm and trying to replace the chocolates he had dislodged with her other hand. 'Sorry, sorry, he's not usually up and about this early—'

'It's absolutely fine, ma'am, please—' Milli scrambled to fix the display, 'don't worry about it. Don't worry about it at all,' she repeated, holding the mother's gaze. 'Really. It's my job.'

'I'm sorry,' the woman said again, but she visibly relaxed, tucking the small boy against her neck and he began to quieten down. She rocked him a little, while Milli reassembled the display. 'We never leave the house this early, when he's so energetic and I'm so—' she gave a one-armed shrug, 'but his father gets home today and he's even more excited than usual.'

'I completely understand,' Milli smiled, something tightening in her chest. 'I know if it were my dad on that plane at his age, I ... ' she trailed off, focusing her efforts instead on fixing the last box of chocolates into the display. 'I'd be over the moon,' she finished, quirking a grin at the woman.

'Oh, he is. For sure,' the woman laughed. She rose to her feet, holding the boy against her hip. He peered curiously at Milli. She waved at him a little awkwardly. She liked kids, but never knew exactly where she stood with them. As he broke out into a shy smile, she figured she hadn't mortally offended him.

The woman looked at the clock behind Milli's head, her eyes widening. 'Would you look at the time?' she asked the boy, her voice climbing in pitch as she adopted an exaggeratedly excited tone. 'Daddy's plane should be here in ten minutes. Ten minutes, Daksh! Are you excited?' The boy giggled, giving a little crow as he mimicked her excited face.

'Thank you again,' the woman told Milli over her shoulder as she made her way back to the gate, bouncing the child on her hip.

Settling back down behind the counter, Milli couldn't focus on the climactic end of her novel. As good as it was, she was more fascinated by the scene playing out in front of her. Daksh and his mother, secure in their little world built for three, waiting for the remaining part of their whole to arrive.

Milli had never known a happy family personally, no matter how many of them she had seens milling back and forth through the airport over the years. Her own father had disappeared before Milli could hold any memories of him in her head, fond or otherwise. It had just been she, her mother and her brother, splintering and fracturing and coming back together. Milli and her mum didn't see eye to eye on most things, and it had been Karan's presence that had held them together for so long. Now, with his passing, there was very little to hold their fractured family together. Just a house they could barely afford even with both their salaries combined and the shared burden of keeping each other alive.

But the love between this woman and her husband had made a child like Daksh utterly carefree and glowing with joy even at this early hour. It was a kind of love that Milli could barely comprehend. Certainly, it was nothing like the passionate embraces that the characters in her favourite novels shared. No, this love was something stronger; somehow, more real. But it was a love which Milli knew she would never know.

Milli believed in love like that with her whole heart; in true, abiding love that built lives instead of consuming them like wildfire. She would be foolish not to believe in what she saw every day. She saw it in the world around her and envied it where it grew. But she didn't expect to experience that kind of love herself. Every day, she resigned herself a little more to a life as a background character, watching as the people around her achieved their happy endings and flew off into the sunset, wrapped in each other's arms. Most days, she could grin and bear it. But today, it settled like a heavy weight on her heart.

The novel was no longer providing an adequate distraction from her thoughts, so she cast it aside and picked up her cell phone instead. Her Facebook was a barrage of messages she didn't want to read. There were the last of the half-hearted notes of sympathy from acquaintances and friends, and the rest of her inbox was swamped with Rahull's private messages, bombarding her with invitations to dinner and offering her a shoulder to cry on, as though he could ever understand what she really needed.

She idly dreamed of blocking him, of spamming them all and hopping on the first plane to wherever that her meagre pay cheque would get her, but she knew she wouldn't be able to go far enough to escape them. Clearing her notifications from the app and resolving to check it only once the day was over, she let herself sink into her latest distraction: Clikrr.

She had downloaded Clikrr one morning when Harman, in prime form, had declared that her never-do-well sister had just gone on a fourth date with a man she had met on the app, and insisting that Milli get on that bandwagon as well. Harman had basically created Milli's profile for her, even posing Milli for the selfie that she would use as her profile picture and writing her bio.

While Milli didn't think that 'Milli. 24. Reader and Dreamer.' summed up much of her life in a way that would interest anyone, it seemed to be just mysterious enough to attract some of the right kind of attention. A couple of men had messaged her already. They had been cute, smart, and interesting enough to pass the time, although not interesting enough for her to agree to meet in person. Even better, they were from far enough away that Milli hadn't grown up with them and watched them through every awkward teenage phase. Clikrr might have been a time-waster, but at least it was a time-waster that allowed her to escape the goldfish bowl of her own life. And besides, as Harman had said, if even her useless sister could find a man on the site, it wouldn't be hard for Milli to find the prince charming that Harman was always insisting she would.

Milli filtered through profiles, swiping left and right, looking more for the sheer monotonous distraction the app provided than for any actual romance. Left on Roshan, 34, holding a cigarette in his mouth. Nope. Left on Rohan, 28, whose profile picture was of a sports car he had obviously lifted from Google Images and had never touched in real life. Right on Ritesh, a 31-year-old football player whose picture was artfully unposed and taken somewhere during a through-hike of some wild jungle trail. He might have something clever to say. Left on Jitender, on Ishan, on Padam, right on Armik and Monty. Nobody had bitten yet, but Milli was confident they would. So long as their name wasn't Rahull, she wouldn't mind chatting with them for a bit either.

Left on Arun, on Rajan, on Sumit and on Vikas. Another two lefts and she was ready to close out of the app when a name came up on her screen that stopped her cold. No profile picture, but located in Chandigarh, apparently less than eight kilometres away from her current location. That was nice. Description: 'Poet in the fast lane. Lover of fine cuisine and oil paints. Looking for a girl along for the ride.' 29 years old. Name: Karan.

On any other day, she wouldn't have given it a second thought. She would have skipped over a man without a profile picture in a heartbeat and spent the day in a fruitless chat with jungle trail boy until the line at work got too busy for her to play games on her phone. But so soon after her brother's death, having a man come into her life who shared her brother's name didn't feel like something she could brush off. Karan. Poet in the fast lane. She found his lack of profile picture mysterious, but wondered if it might be just the kind of mystery she needed. She swiped right.

A cheer went up from Gate F10. Milli raised her head in time to see a blur of camouflage as a man swept up the woman from earlier into his arms, kissing her soundly on the mouth. Her young son wrapped his arms tightly around the man's leg. The boy's father grinned, breaking apart from the woman in order to pick him up and hoist him onto his shoulders. The little boy wrapped his arms around the soldier's neck as he leaned in to give the woman another kiss.

Milli's eyes welled with tears as she watched their reunion. She couldn't help but think about what might have been if her brother hadn't died. The family he might have built to greet him at the gate. If nothing else, she could have been there to welcome him home, alive and breathing, instead of wrapped in a flag and tucked into a coffin. She was happy for the woman and her husband, happy to see Daksh reunited with his father, happy to see their picture complete and their love for each other in spite of all the hardships the soldier had weathered at the border. But it still hurt her. That should have been Karan's story, too. And now it never would be.

She couldn't cry for him. Not at the counter where anyone could see. Not in an airport bustling with people, all of them happy for the couple at the gate. No one would understand her tears. So she held them in, remembering Harman's words, and let a smile, wide and sincere, bloom across her face. She gave a little cheer and a thumbs up to the woman as she shouldered her husband's carry-on, insisting that he carry little Daksh instead. The woman waved back, mouthing 'thank you' on her way out of the airport. Milli continued to smile long after the family disappeared towards the baggage claim.

Her phone buzzed, and she looked down reflexively, prepared to tell Rahull off for good this time. It was as though a crack had formed in her soul from the pressure she had put herself under to conceal and keep any emotion she might have truly felt off her face. She wasn't sure that she could keep herself from exploding now if anyone tried to talk to her.

But it wasn't Rahull. Her Clikrr showed a new message from Karan. Milli chuckled in spite of herself. The man certainly had interesting timing. She could give him that if nothing else. As the screen loaded on his message, she glanced up at the now parting crowd. The constant shifting of the airport had already moved on, as though the couple who had just been reunited had never been there at all. Milli wished that she could move on so easily.

How is a lovely lady like yourself doing on such a fine day as this one? Karan's message read. She blushed a little, but couldn't keep herself from rolling her eyes. Clearly the man fancied himself a perfect gentleman. On any other day, she might have responded in kind, starting a fancy flirtation that led nowhere and disappointed them both. But she didn't have it in her heart. She felt trapped by her feelings. If he wanted to know how she was doing, she would tell him.

Honestly? She typed back. His reply was immediate.

Honestly. I wouldn't have said it if I didn't mean it.

Have you ever been alone in a crowd of people? Have you ever been trapped by other people's expectations? Have people insisted that you ought to smile and act like nothing's wrong when you can see the world crashing down on you? Now that she had started, Milli couldn't seem to stop. *And if you have, how do you manage to do it? Because I'm here in the middle of a hurricane and I seem to be the only person who can feel that it's raining.*

Karan didn't respond for a long moment. 'Ha,' Milli said to herself with a note of bitter satisfaction. 'I knew I'd be too much for him.' But just as she was about to put her phone away, it buzzed again with a message from Karan.

I know you won't believe me, it said, *but you've described the way I feel all the time. I don't know what to tell you – the painted-on smile I wear is so fixed on my face that I'm not sure I could cry if I wanted to. I can't tell you what to do, other than to say 'don't do what I've done,' but I can say that I'm here to offer an umbrella to you if it's raining where you are. Tell me whatever you need to say.*

This time the smile on Milli's face crept up without her knowledge. It was the first one she hadn't had to paste on in some time.

Thank you for that offer. She typed back. *Really, it means more than I could ever say.*

Of course. Any time.

Can we start over? She asked.

Sure. Be as honest as you need. How are you doing today?

Not well. We cremated my brother more than a month ago but every day still feels like the day I found out that he died. She typed. She backspaced another couple of lines before adding: *But I met someone who made me smile in spite of it, so I guess it isn't all bad.*

I'm sorry to hear that, about your brother. But glad to hear you smiled.

Me too, she responded, and was surprised to find that the smile was still on her face. *And how are you today?* She asked him. It took him a moment to respond.

Honestly?

Honestly.

The cursor blinked as the man began to type. Milli was a little shocked to realize how interested she was in his answer. She was glad she had taken the risk and contacted him. Maybe, she thought to herself, this awful day wasn't a total waste after all.

THREE

The moonlight shone like silver through the window, casting a glow around the darkened bedroom. It looked cosy enough, but, despite the spring weather and the plush luxury of the bed, Karan felt cold all over. What good were high thread counts and silk sheets if they couldn't keep him warm? He adjusted his position gingerly as he flipped the page on his novel, his eyes blurring the paragraph in front of him. Pain spread across his hip with the movement. He exhaled a steady breath through his nose while he waited for the pain to pass. As the world came back into soft focus, the lulling, vapid monologue of Prachi's thoughts about their upcoming vacation to Bora Bora sharpened abruptly.

'Karan,' his girlfriend snapped, padding over to the bed from her position at the vanity, fanning her hand to dry her nails. She lay a manicured hand across the open face of his book, blocking his view of the page with her fingers. 'Bora Bora? The packing list? I need you to be listening to me.'

'I'm listening,' he gritted out, knowing he would really rather be doing anything but listening. The edge of a whine in her voice let him know that if he didn't at least put up a convincing front, she would spend the rest of the night sulking, making the already cold room absolutely frigid. His eyes flickered over her, noting with approval the way her silk robe slipped off her smooth skin, exposing the curve of her breast. She clearly revelled in his interest.

A pleased expression fell over her face as she leaned forward into his space with a Cheshire cat grin.

'I'm sorry, is there something distracting you from me?' She asked with a wicked smile that transitioned into an exaggerated pout as he snatched his book away from her painted claws. 'I want your attention,' she said pointedly, tracing a finger across the line of his exposed stomach on the bed. 'Your full attention.' Her hands dipped lower, teasing him as she folded her fingers over the waistband of his boxers. He slid up the bed, trying to ignore the pain that crept up his legs.

'You've got my attention, babe,' he told her, gesturing pointedly at his lap. 'Fully.'

She gave him a dry, false grin. 'Somehow, I don't think so.' With that, she let her robe fall to the floor.

Prachi began to move her hips in a sinuous motion, arching her back and running her hands through her hair. She hummed a little to music only she could hear, giving Karan a beseeching look through her lashes as she danced. As he suspected, there was nothing but inviting, sun kissed skin and toned muscle under the silk robe she discarded on the carpet. He appreciated her form even if he could appreciate little else about her. Prachi was fit, golden and tanned from hours spent sunning herself at the beach with some fruity tropical drink Karan purchased for her in one hand and a vacuous fashion magazine in the other. Her dark hair curled loosely at her shoulder blades, moving like a waterfall as she tossed it back, giving a beckoning shimmy of her hips. She might not be much of a reader, but Prachi's body was poetry in motion.

'Is this helping you focus on what's important?' She asked him with a prizewinning smile, as though she really thought she had won something in capturing Karan's attention with the movement of her body. And Karan couldn't help but think that she had. There in that sensuous swing of her hips she held Karan's fortune at the mercy of her whims. But Karan's world was a cold one, and it would be a lot colder without Prachi in it. Besides, Prachi was capable of doing what few girls could: the moment she undid his buttons and discovered that there was more to him than fast cars and credit cards, she didn't run screaming although she was revolted by the broad scars across his chest. She merely skirted around the angry welts with her hands and turned a blind eye to them.

Prachi was more than a pretty face. She was a convincing actress too. She had carefully schooled the look of disgust off her face at the sight of the puffy, precise surgical scars which Karan kept hidden. The marks left over from his miracle cure had become the bane of his existence, keeping love at bay. It was as though when they had gone in for a valve replacement in his teenage years, the surgeons had inadvertently excised his whole heart, leaving an empty hole in its place which no amount of fast cars, glittering nights of luxury and beautiful women like Prachi could fill.

The ones that didn't balk at the sight of his scars tried to play nursemaid with him, which was altogether intolerable in a way that being rejected never had been. Solitude was preferable to smothering, he supposed. The flavour of pity in their kisses nauseated Karan. Prachi might have been an actress, but at least she made no pretence of trying to comfort him about his health. She was cold and indifferent and shamelessly open about using his fortune for whatever held her interest that day, but she was incredible in the sack and sometimes witty enough to talk to after they had had sex. He didn't love her, but he recognized that she was worth keeping by his side.

He supposed that that was why he had kept her around for so long, even when she came in late smelling of another man's cologne and drunk off expensive champagne with her panty hose ripped, rolling her eyes as she deflected his questions like the whole thing was an amusing joke he hadn't gotten yet. 'Please don't tell me we're supposed to be exclusive now, Karan, I think you know me better than that after all this time ...' she would say with that teasing, plastic grin on her face. Although she kept collecting a lot of jewellery from Tiffany and Cartier on Karan's cards, she'd never asked for a ring. The one time he had offered, she had laughed in his face, telling him she hadn't thought he was a 'marriage kind of a boy.' He might know her, but it was clear she barely knew him at all.

However, after that incident, he had downloaded a dating app called Clickrr, more to pass the time when Prachi really pissed him off than out of any serious expectations of finding love. It was an innocent enough way to daydream about finding a woman whose interest went beyond his wallet and into his soul. If he ever found one, he promised himself, he would leave Prachi wherever it was they happened to be at the time. Perhaps she would be happy in Bora Bora, drink in her hand and no real responsibility. Perhaps she wouldn't even notice he was gone.

She danced at the foot of the bed, undulating like a wave as she gyrated, the song in her mind slow enough to be a funeral dirge. *Get on with it*, Karan couldn't help but think, a little meanly. She wouldn't be satisfied until they were wheels-up and on their way towards someplace warm enough and so far away that she could do as she pleased without consequence. But she would find some way to distract herself with Karan until she could distract herself with something else. And Karan wasn't opposed to being used anymore. Prachi was hot, and Karan was so cold.

'C'mon then,' he huffed, 'get on with it.' The ringing laughter in his ear as she crawled up the bed towards him was sharp and a little cruel, but to Karan's lonely heart, it felt like a glimmer of gold in the chilly evening air. It wasn't much, but it was enough for now.

———•———

As the temporary reprieve of ecstasy drained from Karan's body, he was left with a nagging ache in his hips that drifted in insidious little tendrils across the expanse of his body. Twisting to escape it merely intensified the pain. The room was silent enough that Karan could hear the pervasive ticking of his aortic valve, but as the pain in his hips flared, a rushing sound like the roar of a jet plane flooded his ears.

The lazy hand that Prachi always rested against his hipbone after they had had sex – soft enough against his skin to be seemingly accidentally positioned, but far enough away from his scars that he knew it was deliberate – generally didn't bother him. But the pain it caused was too much tonight. Restless and cold, his chest felt suddenly tight. He had to escape the stifling room. He moved her hand, placed it on the coverlet and stood up slowly in a movement that ached all the way until its completion.

'Where do you think you're going?' she asked, her voice husky with sleep and satisfaction.

'Taking a drive,' he responded shortly, pulling on his t-shirt. 'Don't wait up.'

Prachi shifted on her elbows until she was sitting up, looking at him. 'Are you taking the Audi or the Porsche?' she asked with genuine curiosity.

'Porsche,' he decided. She perked up a little, no doubt remembering how quickly he could whip his Cayenne GTS on the beautiful, winding backwoods of rural Chandigarh. Before she could invite herself along, Karan asked her a question that stopped her cold.

'If I didn't have any money, would you even be here? Would you have hung around for so long? Would you have even spoken to me at all?'

The false, over-bright smile that she flashed him told him everything he needed to know. 'Oh, honey—' she began, but he didn't stick around to listen to whatever noncommittal answer she was attempting to give him.

Taking his keys from the nightstand and sliding them into the back pocket of his jeans in a fluid motion that made his aching legs protest, he made his way down the flight of stairs and through the east wing in the relative darkness and quiet. The waitstaff who lived on the property had turned in for the night so Karan was left alone with his thoughts as he keyed in the entrance code to the garage and slid behind the wheel of the Porsche, opening the garage door and rolling out into the night.

Driving gave Karan a deep sense of peace that he couldn't find in painting or poetry. Not even sleep made him feel as relaxed and focused as sliding behind the wheel of one of his cars. There was no darkness anywhere like there was in these parts, pitch black and heavy as lead with humidity. On the other hand, there was no night as bright with stars as a Chandigarh night, either. All the lights from the homes of the few old timers who still lived in this suburbia had long since blinked out, giving the milky way unimpeded leeway to shine above him. The air was cool against his skin as he cracked the windows.

He wanted to whoop for joy, feeling the freedom he hadn't felt all day as his foot fell heavy on the gas pedal. The suburbs gave way to country roads as the pitch black of well past midnight turned into the grey of earliest morning. Dawn hadn't quite broken, but the sky was preparing to house the sun. Still nothing, man or animal, stirred. There was not a person on these black back roads at this hour. Karan was free to explore his own thoughts.

But his thoughts these days were as dangerous as the winding roads he drove down and they took as dark a turn. The persistent ache in his hips felt like the monster under his bed, ready to reach out and claim him. Hadn't he suffered enough? Most of his early memories were of hospital wallpaper and putting on a brave face while samples of his blood were taken and shots administered. He hadn't even graduated high school before he first under went the knife for a valve replacement, something that most men never had to worry about until after they had retired. And this pain, what would it mean for him? What had once been a dull ache sharpened painfully, and Karan knew his body well enough to know that it wouldn't get any better. He had already been through hell. He didn't know how much further he could descend.

The shadow of ramshackle houses hove into view here and there, so far away from anything more than a general store and a fast food quick stop that it would be a ghost town within the next decade. Many of the houses here were already abandoned or else inhabited by old folks too stubborn to be moved out of them. This was despite the fact that a single inspection would label every house in the town unfit for human habitation. He felt much the same as those houses – too desolate for anything to live safely within him. He couldn't remember feeling any differently. It was strange – his own home was a lavish mansion full of every pleasure a person could want. So how was it that he felt this strange kinship with these houses?

As he rounded a curve, a house he hadn't noticed before came into view, illuminated and warm-looking. It was dilapidated, sure, but it looked as though its inhabitants were still trying. There was a little garden patch on the grass and clothes on the line. *That's the kind of house a person might actually dream of living in*, Karan thought to himself, *that's the kind of house that looks like home.*

He was struck by the strange urge to pull off, go up the gravel driveway and knock on the door. He felt as though it would be warm in there, like there would be someone waiting on the other side of the door to hand him a cup of coffee and enquire how his drive had been. The thought of his own mansion and Prachi sulking behind the door didn't make him want to drive any faster. Instead he slowed, enjoying the sight of the house in his rear-view mirror until he rounded another bend and it disappeared for good.

Feeling oddly as though he had made a wrong turn somewhere, Karan shifted his foot back onto the gas pedal and drove off into the night.

———•———

There were few moments more enjoyable in Milli's life than the ones she stole for herself when she worked the morning shift. She would wake up so early in the morning that it was the middle of the night, while her mother was still too high to stir from her position on the couch, so she could finish her chores before she had to run for work. Milli would sneak out onto the porch while the laundry machine spun her clothes clean with a cup of hot black coffee and stare up at the Chandigarh night sky, head tilted back to bask in the galactic display. Alone with her thoughts and the chatter of tree frogs in the dark, Milli felt she could be on the precipice of something good, almost falling only to find she had been able to fly the whole time. What might have been a shooting star but was probably an airplane carved a straight path through the dark, blinking all the way. Knowing it was silly and doing it anyway, Milli squeezed her eyes shut, thinking to herself, *I wish, I wish, I wish.*

In front of her closed eyelids, she saw a sudden brightness. Her eyes blinking open, she was momentarily caught in the beam of headlights of a passing car. She had never seen anyone driving on this road this late. Perhaps it was an omen, some kind of a sign that the wish she had made would come true. For a moment, she fantasized that the car might turn up her driveway and take her away from this place, her mother still passed out on the couch with the pill bottle slipping out of her hand. But the car turned the corner and vanished. Milli sighed, letting her eyes drift close once more. *I wish, I wish, I wish.*

Four

Milli's mother awoke from a dead sleep to dense smoke filling the room. Milli had been staring vacantly at the skillet of scrambled eggs starting to smoke on the stove. Her mother's loud swearing snapped her back to life, and she dumped the contents of the skillet into the trash can. Milli's mother rolled over, blinking irritably in the dim morning light.

'Why have you made such a mess?' she grunted, wiping a hand over her mouth. Milli quietly filled a glass of water and set it down next to her mother on the coffee table. She didn't expect a thank you and her mother didn't give her one. It was reprieve enough for the long morning she had had when her phone buzzed again. Karan. He had contacted her just a couple of hours before, asking if she was awake early enough to see the sunrise. Milli, her back aching as she bent over a load of laundry that needed folding, was afraid that her response of *I often see it and rarely enjoy it*, would drive him away. But Karan had merely told her, *I appreciate the honesty*, and changed the topic to the beautiful weather coming up for the weekend.

Pity I won't be able to enjoy it.

He had just sent her. *Why not?*

She responded, *fresh air is great if you can get it.*

'Your face is gonna split in two if you keep smiling like that,' her mother yawned, tightening the ribbon on her stained pyjama bottoms as she struggled to her feet. Her cheeks were unnaturally flushed already. The water sat untouched on the table. 'Who are you texting this early in the morning?'

'No one, Ma,' Milli rolled her eyes. Her hands cupped protectively around her phone. She grabbed a box of cereal and poured a measure into the bowl. Her eyes were on the clock as she moved through the kitchen. 'Just a friend from work.'

Her mother either didn't hear her or didn't care enough to respond. She rifled through the cabinets looking for something, although Milli couldn't say what it was. Clearly, she didn't find what she was looking for and she mumbled something under her breath, shuffling off to the bathroom. Milli smoothed the line of her work shirt with one hand as she shovelled a spoonful of sugary cereal into her mouth. Her phone buzzed.

Fresh air in another country has all the same benefits as the fresh air here, or so I've been told.

A pang of jealousy filled Milli's stomach. It was an ugly feeling, unbecoming of the woman she wanted to be, so she smothered it with another spoonful of sugary cereal as she typed out her response.

Air pollution is a global problem. Which other country?

There was a blood-curdling thunk from the bathroom, followed by her mother swearing profanely as the toilet made a pathetic gurgling sound. 'Milli! Milli Bajwa! Get yourself in here and help your mother!'

Milli sighed, shovelling in a final desperate spoonful of cereal as she sat her phone on the table and went to see what her mother had managed to do this time. She opened the door to find her mother with her pyjama bottoms around her ankles, holding a cracked piece of porcelain from the washbasin which had broken almost neatly in two. The pipes were still running, water spraying across the floor.

'I don't know what I've done!' her mother swore, but the spilled pills dissolving in the sink water on the linoleum told Milli all she needed to know. Turning off the tap, she took the piece from her mother and set it on the floor, salvaging what pills she could from the mess on the ground and dropping bath towels to soak up the water.

'I'm gonna be late for work, Ma,' Milli sighed, taking an ineffectual swipe at the mess with her foot as she examined the damage done to the sink. 'And if I lose my job, there's no way we can afford to pay for repairs.'

'Oh, we can't afford to pay for repairs anyway,' her mother hissed, as though Milli was the one who had broken the basin. 'Doesn't matter what you do. If we had a man to come around the old place ever so often, it might be a different story. Someone who knew how to fix stuff up.'

'I don't wanna hear it, please, just go sit on the couch and let me take care of this mess,' Milli said, her hands fluttering in frustration. 'Just sit down and let me—'

'It was so much better when Karan was still here,' Milli's mother sighed. The sorrow that had turned her to pills in the first place now seeped into her face like the water through the cracks in the broken basin. 'Always thought he would have been more useful if your dad had stuck around to teach him a thing or two, but even then he turned out alright.'

'He was a fine man, Ma, but can you please go in the kitchen while I fix this mess?' Milli bit her lip, hoping tears wouldn't well in her eyes. Whenever her mother took to thinking about her brother's passing this early in the day, she was more of a mess than Milli could handle when she returned home in the evening, tired from her day at work. Coming home to scrub vomit off the floor wasn't her idea of a relaxing evening, but she had to prepare for the inevitable. Hiding the bottle didn't work, and neither did pouring it down the now demolished sink. The day was ruined before it even began.

'I had a dream about him last night,' her mother was babbling, 'and he said we ought to get some new man around here to help us.'

Milli couldn't help but scoff. The sound made her mother's face turn red with fury. 'You can laugh at me if you want, Milli Bajwa, but I know what I heard. It was like an omen.'

'Please, you haven't had a dream that you could remember ever since you cracked open the pill bottle,' Milli rolled her eyes, sweeping bits of porcelain off the floor with her hand.

'That boy Rahull's nice enough,' Milli's mother said, wide-eyed as though the thought had just struck her, when in reality she had been bugging Milli about Rahull for years. 'Big boy. Big hands. And a steady job too. He works hard, Milli. Not like those boys in your story books with soft hands and tragic pasts. Rahull's a steady boy who would do us all right.'

'You like him so much, you marry him,' Milli gritted, straightening. Her work shirt was soaked and sprinkled with porcelain from the broken sink, but it would dry on her way to work.

'Since your brother died, we need a man to come and do what—' Milli's mother began again. It made something snap inside of Milli.

'Don't you ever, ever, imply that any other man in the world could replace my brother. Don't you ever!' she shouted. Then, with a cut off swear, she realized how much time had passed. 'Now look what you've done. I'm going to be late for work,' she rushed to the kitchen table, snatching her phone and her keys off the table. 'Don't break anything else while I'm gone, Ma, we can't afford it.'

And with that she let the screen door on the front porch slam shut, taking the stairs two at a time down to where her sedan was parked in the grass. After two false starts, the car came to life with a roar. The dashboard clock flickered on, letting Milli know that she had twenty-one minutes to make a drive that usually took forty-seven minutes in good traffic. She didn't even bother to curse, resigned to the fate that today was going to be a bad day no matter what she did.

―――――•―――――

It wasn't until she was stuck in the gridlocked Chandigarh traffic, already more than half an hour late for work, that she remembered seeing the notification for Karan's message on her phone. The thought filled her with the first sense of happiness she hadn't felt since her cup of coffee at the break of dawn that morning.

Was going to be in Bora Bora, but there's been a change of plans. I suppose I could go anywhere. The first message said. Since that one, he had sent two more.

Looks like the next international flight of interest to me is heading to Paris. There's a hotel there I absolutely adore, there near the Arc de Triomphe. Thinking about making a getaway there.

Most puzzling of all, his last message read only: *I've never been more afraid to fly.*

Milli puzzled over this final message, knowing it couldn't be meant for her. Finally, she wrote back, choosing her words carefully, *not sure about the air quality in Paris. What do you mean? Nervous flier?*

It took Karan only seconds to reply back, *not a nervous flier. At least, I haven't been before. But everything's different now. I'm different. And I'm afraid this might be my la*

The text cut off mid-word as though he hadn't meant to send it. Milli wasn't sure what to do. Should she ignore it or try to find out what he meant? Her phone buzzed again before she could say anything else.

Well, I'll be stuck in the airport for the next twenty minutes before they start boarding, but I'm getting on the plane. Ticket bought. Fear overcome. Apologies for my momentary cowardice. I'm not usually like this.

Milli quite liked the way a man like Karan confessed his fears to her. In fact, she found she rather preferred his honesty to Rahull's machismo and boorish bravado. She had never met a man who shared his true feelings with her. It was like something out of a story book. A fantasy come to life.

What is it you're always saying? That you can take my honesty? Why can't I return the favour this time?

Karan's response didn't come through for a long time. In fact, she was almost to the parking lot by the time her phone buzzed again.

Sometimes honesty is hard. But I'll do my best for you.

What an odd, wonderful man, Milli thought to herself, shutting off the engine and stumbling towards the airport entrance. She was so late at this point, she was sure she would be written up. However, they were too short-staffed to suspend her, thank God for small favours; but they might fire her if it happened again. Still, even with the threat of discipline hanging over her, she couldn't help but linger by the Air France desk, hoping to catch a glimpse of the mysterious man.

However, it was far too late by the time she got to the counter. Although the flight to Paris had taken off only a few minutes earlier, it had been boarded almost half an hour ago. Still, she couldn't help but marvel. A man who wanted to give her his honesty and time, who promised he would do his best for her, had been in the airport only two metres away from where Milli worked every day. Her eyes scanned the terminal in every slow moment she got throughout her day, envisaging what he looked like, where he had been sitting, if he knew that Milli had been almost close enough to call his name.

'You're in a weirdly good mood,' Harman noted. It wasn't quite a criticism, but Milli ignored it anyway. She was having trouble controlling the expression on her face. A smile burst through against her will.

'I suppose I am,' she teased, trying to seem coy. She was torn between wanting to gush and tell Harman everything and needing to keep this one kind man, this small miracle, to herself. In the end, Harman didn't ask, and that allowed Milli to keep her secret for now.

'Me too, girl,' Harman said, 'I'm in a good mood too. I just saw the funniest thing at the Jet Desk and I'm still rolling on the floor laughing about it. You would not believe it if I told you. Go on, guess. You're not gonna get it.'

Milli threw her hands up in the air, miming defeat. 'You've got me. I couldn't possibly guess.'

Harman shot her a conspiratorial look and leaned in closer, 'So this rich girl comes up to the desk and she's trying to print out her boarding pass, only to find out that her flight has been cancelled. She's all dolled up and everything too, says she's meeting someone there, there must be some mistake, don't they know who she is, et cetera—' Harman threw her head back and guffawed heartily. 'Like anyone knows who she is. I sure didn't.'

'I doubt I would either,' Milli allowed.

'Girl, you wouldn't know a Kareena Kapoor from Shah Rukh Khan,' Harman teased. 'So she's throwing this honest-to-God hissy fit. Stomps her feet in these teetering stilettos, almost trips in the process. Turns out her boyfriend's cancelled not only her flight, but the credit card she used of his!'

'Guess that's one way to dump someone,' Milli said quietly, her mind racing. Was it connection or coincidence?

'And you'll never guess where the girl was going, either,' Harman cackled. 'Bora Bora. Seriously, she's whining about how she should be on the beach right now while I'm spraying down the desk, thinking to myself, You're the biggest bore-a I've ever heard in my life!

Her mirth at her own little pun was contagious and Milli couldn't help but crack a smile in response. The mystery of the day had just gotten more mysterious. She wanted to message Karan to see what he had to say about it, but she figured by now he was up in the air, a thousand kilometres above their heads, hurtling towards some place he actually wanted to be. She hoped there was no fear left in his heart.

She felt a little jealous of his freedom, his ability to travel as he pleased, to go where he wanted, but the feeling couldn't stick. So, she laughed along with Harman. Everything else could wait.

———◆———

Since Karan's flight touched down in Paris, it was as though he had taken up residence in Milli's phone. She envied his ability to leave for the sake of leaving, to arrive in Paris for no other reason than the sheer delight of being somewhere that wasn't his home and experiencing a culture unlike anything he knew. Even so, he offered Milli her own little escape in the form of the messages he sent to her. Through the images, video and texts full of poetic descriptions of the city of lights, Milli felt as though she were by his side, seeing Paris with her own eyes instead of just through her phone. Art in the Louvre. Cajun food in the 3rd arrondissement. Street musicians playing jazz. The Eiffel Tower at night.

The way people milled about the city, lovers holding hands and tourists snapping photos with disposable cameras, was enchanting to Milli. The water flowing through the Seine wasn't as filthy as she had been led to imagine, although Karan told her that it certainly didn't smell of roses. The ancient architecture juxtaposed against contemporary pieces gave Milli the impression of a city alive and breathing, one that had existed forever and would continue to exist into eternity. She was in love.

The pictures don't do it justice, Karan told her. *I know it's hard to believe, but it's even more beautiful in person.*

I'll take your word for it. I'm happy to experience it this way for now.

Experiencing Paris through Karan's texts felt like the closest she would ever get to beauty. Looking in the mirror, her face looked tired and strange. She had had rough days one after another that felt like they would never end. There was a pile of dishes in the kitchen sink that weren't getting any cleaner, and there was no replacement basin for the bathroom anywhere in the foreseeable future. Milli had not budgeted for it. The income simply wasn't there.

She had considered breaking into the savings that she had squirreled away in an old jar in her bedroom for the washbasin, but once again resolved that the money was for her on the day she escaped this life. She had seen her mother spitting toothpaste onto the dirty dishes, but had been too tired for the fight that would have ensued had she tried to admonish her. No, the money in the jar was for escaping the world where people spat toothpaste into dirty sinks. Not for buying back into it.

Supper. That was the one thing she could do for herself that might make a little bit of a difference. She was miserable and hungry. She couldn't do anything about the misery besides cling desperately to her phone and hope Karan would send something lovely her way soon. He had fallen asleep a few hours ago and she had been alone with her thoughts for too long now. But she could fix hungry, or at least she could if there was anything in the fridge.

She had her head in the refrigerator, when she heard her phone go off. It was Karan, accompanied by a picture of a croissant stuffed with chocolate, a bowl of fresh fruit, and a steaming cup of black coffee. The image of the food against the soft white sheets and rumpled comforter suggesting he hadn't yet made it out of bed was accompanied by the text, *I had breakfast in bed in Paris this morning. Wish you had been here.*

And what was Milli supposed to do with that, she wondered, trying to coach the blush off her face through sheer force of will as she avoided thinking about the mess he had made of the sheets. Sometimes he was just so charming, as if saying the right thing in the right moment came as naturally to him as breathing. Goodness. She felt both flustered and pleased.

Wish I were there too. Dinner is a bust tonight.

She settled her hand on the styrofoam egg carton, settling for a fried egg sandwich and giving up on thinking of anything more elaborate for supper. It wasn't an appetising thought, but it was better than the hunger she could feel gnawing in her gut. She sat the yellow carton on the counter with a sigh, glaring at it as though it were her worst enemy. Her phone buzzed again.

What's wrong with dinner?

Maybe I can help?

Milli huffed a laugh. *From France? I don't even think you can order a pizza.*

His answer came more quickly than she expected.

I think we can do a little better than pizza, even with the distance between us. What food are we working with?

Eggs and little else. I was going to make a fried egg sandwich and call it a day. I'm exhausted, honestly. Work was hard, home is harder. You've been the only nice part of my day.

Karan's response was comforting and sweet. Milli smiled reading it. *Send me a list of what we've got to work with. I'm gonna cook you the best meal you've ever eaten. And it'll be easy, too. I promise you won't be any more tired than you would be if you made the fried egg sandwich.*

I trust you, she told him, no longer trying to fight down the smile on her face. It had been a losing battle from the beginning when it came to trying to keep her composure regarding Karan. She opened the refrigerator door, peering at its contents with disdain and no small amount of disgust.

'Let's see,' she muttered under her breath, typing as she went. Eggs and eggs galore, some wilted parsley, bought for some purpose Milli couldn't remember. Three tupperware containers with spoiled leftovers that Milli couldn't bring herself to clean. Orange juice and milk, some hard-white cheese that was turning blue around the edges. She could trim that, she figured. Lunch meat. Ham. The last quarter of a loaf of bread. The end of a stick of butter. A raw onion. Ketchup, mustard, mayonnaise.

And that's it, she texted him. *There's nothing edible in the freezer.*

He might have appreciated the honesty but she wasn't yet brave enough to tell him that two days ago, her mother had been so high she had forgotten to shut the freezer door and everything had defrosted and spoiled. Milli had scrubbed for hours, desperate to remove any trace of the mess from the cracked floor.

Frittata, he responded decidedly, faster than Milli might have thought he would. *Takes twenty minutes and tastes great. Got any garlic?*

Only the powdered kind.

A pinch of that will do. Can you peel and dice the onion for me? Chew some gum if you have any to prevent tears.

Oh, and turn the broiler on in your oven. You'll need it.

Milli did as she was told, stopping for a moment to fish a bit of spearmint gum out of her purse and pop it into her mouth. She found the process surprisingly pleasant, smiling and humming to herself as she worked under Karan's careful guidance. It was as though someone was cooking for her, watching over her to make sure nothing burned. It was lovely, a bit like being cared for, and Milli hadn't had anyone to care for her in such a long time.

Heat up that butter in the skillet and sauté the onion. While that's going, crack four eggs into a bowl and blend a half pinch of the garlic powder, some salt, and some pepper into them.

Is this mixed enough? Milli accompanied a text with the picture of her bowl. *Ignore the mess in the kitchen please. I didn't make most of it.*

Messy roommates, huh?

Messy mother. She bit her lip, acutely aware that she had never been so honest with anyone before. Not even Rahull, who spent far more time than was healthy hanging around their place, and seemed to know the true extent of how far her mother had fallen.

I'm sorry to hear that. Can you shred some of that ham?

That I can do. Milli worked quickly with the knife, feeling exhaustion seeping out of her bones and something warmer taking its place. She couldn't help but imagine Karan standing over her, watching her work with warm, kind eyes as he advised her on her knife skills and put a pinch of something else into the onions to liven up the taste.

Scraping the ham into the pan with the onions, she gave it a moment to settle as per Karan's instructions before pouring the eggs over the whole mess.

Now, how you cook it is just as important as the ingredients you're cooking with, Karan advised her sagely. *You're going to want to keep lifting the edges of the egg as they cook, letting the uncooked portion of the eggs flow underneath. It's kind of tricky, but I bet you can do it.*

You don't know me very well, she teased him, *I burn water.*

That's just because you haven't had a good teacher yet. Anyone can cook. It just takes time to learn and a passion for the craft. I believe in you. Just lift it as it gets solid and you'll find long before you have an excellent frittata on your hands.

And with his confidence, Milli found that she was doing a pretty remarkable job. The eggs in the skillet turned golden all the way through. Milli sent him a picture of her work.

Awesome. Now, shred a bit of the cheese you've cleaned up into it for a last little kick and you'll be good to put it in the broiler.

When do I get to eat it? I'm hungry. :(

Another couple of minutes. I'll tell you when to take it out.

Milli opened the oven, carefully sliding the skillet between the racks.

Got it in!

Great. Proud of you.

She had never cooked like this before and was amazed she hadn't messed up yet. Karan's instructions were so specific and easy to follow, it was as though he was cooking through her. It was an incredible feeling. If someone had taught her how to cook this way years ago, Milli might not have subsisted on cereal for so long.

Pop it out of the broiler. Make sure you turn the oven off. And voila! Ham frittata, from me to you.

Milli couldn't wait another second to eat. Cutting into the frittata, still steaming and hot, she shovelled a heaped helping onto her plate. The taste was impossible to describe. It was basic, sure, and maybe a little drier than it would have been had Karan made it himself, but with her fork in her mouth she could taste all the care that had gone into the meal. Karan, a world away, had made certain that she was well-fed and happy. Mostly, the people in Milli's life were focused on what she could do for them. To have someone do something for her like that … it was nearly unbelievable.

She sent Karan a picture of the frittata, captioned, *The best thing I've ever eaten.*

Then, before she could talk herself out of it, she turned the camera around and snapped a selfie with a smile on her face. She didn't look so tired with the smile on her face, even without makeup on and her hair loose, curling gently around her shoulders. She was wearing a sweatshirt, but the stain on it was cut off from view. For the first time in, she didn't know how long, Milli actually felt beautiful.

She felt herself poised at a threshold, trying to decide whether to take a step across it into the unknown. Karan seemed to enjoy being a man of mystery, cautious about sharing his face with her even as he bared his soul. If she sent him a picture of her face, would he put an end at once to their little game? Would she be as beautiful as he had pictured her? Surely she envisioned him as handsome beyond belief, but she knew nothing of how he actually appeared. Would she be shattering his illusion, or would he find her face better than anything he could ever dream up?

Milli wasn't a coward. He had sent her so much to enjoy, and while pictures of her little world in shambles wouldn't impress him like the streets of Paris had enchanted her, she could certainly send him a pretty picture of her smiling face to thank him for his kindness to her.

See? I'm smiling.

Karan's response didn't come for a while. She wasn't sure if he was sending her a picture of himself. They hadn't exchanged pictures yet, and she was nervous that she had made a huge gaffe by sending him one. He had essentially cooked her dinner, certainly a picture of her face wouldn't scare him off? Maybe she should have put on makeup and posed carefully. But just as she had worried herself into a frenzy, his response popped up. No picture, just text.

It's a beautiful smile.

She grinned around her last bite of frittata.

It's all for you.

FIVE

The next day, Milli was digging holes for fence posts, working harder on her day off than she did on her days on. It had been her belief growing up that no matter how destroyed a house looked on the inside, it was the outside that mattered. Keeping up appearances was the most important thing a person could do. And since her neighbour's dogs had destroyed their garden just a few weeks ago, a fence needed to be built. As she sunk her shovel deep into the Chandigarh soil, she was glad for the years of labour that had strengthened her arms so that she no longer had to beg for help to get the task done. No one was coming to help her. In any case, she didn't need anyone.

It was barely six thirty in the morning when his latest text had come through: *If you could go anywhere in Paris, where would you go?*

She didn't hesitate. Her answer was always the same. City Lights in San Francisco, The Strand in New York City, Shakespeare and Co. in Paris.

Shakespeare and Co. The bookshop in the 5th arrondissement. I've only ever seen photographs before, but it feels like home to me.

Shakespeare and Co. it is. She had gotten in response, and drifted back off to sleep before she heard anything else. There were no new texts on her phone when she woke up and she had set herself to the nasty physical task at hand before it got too hot to dig more.

Hours later, the midday heat began creeping across her back, staining her flesh pink where the sunscreen had rubbed off. There was no one to help make certain the posts were perpendicular, so she resigned herself to building a cheap and poor-looking fence. She could only hope it was functional. Her muscles burned with the strain from the work she had done. Sweat dripped off her forehead and soaked through her shirt. 'Exhausted' didn't begin to cover how she felt. A headache was smarting at her temples, its steady pounding keeping time with her heartbeat.

Planting her shovel deep into the earth, Milli let out a swear and stalked back into the house. Her face was streaked with dirt, her hair soaked with sweat. She felt a mess and looked it, too. Thank God there was no one around to see her. She snatched up her phone from the table, reading it with a sigh. Two texts from Rahull asking if he could come over, because he knew her mother wasn't home; an email reminding her that the gas bill was late; and seven new notifications from Karan.

It wasn't like him to text her this much. When she opened her phone, she gasped in delight. In her inbox were more pictures of the inside of Shakespeare and Co. than she had seen in her life. A sign over the door reading 'Be Not Inhospitable to Strangers Lest They be Angels in Disguise.' A spiral of books, books piled high on tables, books lining the walls on shelves, books tucked underneath the stairwell even. The old and dimly lit shop seemed to shine with a warmth that Milli craved.

One picture stood out from the rest: it was as though Karan had turned the camera by accident and managed to clip a bit of himself into the frame when he pressed the button. Milli could see the outline of his jaw in the darkness, a shadow of facial hair along the bone there. She wanted to see more … he must have sent the image on purpose. He would reveal the rest of himself to her in good time.

The fantasy of exploring Paris with Karan became different after seeing that image. Picnics under the Eiffel Tower and walks along the river became interspersed with fantasies of a more private nature, of sneaking off into a secluded corner of Shakespeare and Co. and pressing a line of kisses against his jawline, books completely forgotten. She felt a little guilty for thinking of him so much in a way he might not return, but it was a pleasant distraction on a hot day as she sunk fence post after fence post and then began work on the fence, unrolling barbed wire with gloved hands. It was a soft fantasy that made her hard reality more bearable.

By the time she finished the fence, the exhaustion deep seated in her bones made it hard to think of anything, fantasy or reality. Although the sun hadn't set yet, Milli picked up her phone from the counter, got out of her filthy work clothes, and sank between her sheets without bothering to do more than turn out the light. She would regret not showering in the morning, she knew, but the thought of having to stand for another minute was unbearable. Still, she hadn't asked anyone for help and that mattered most to her.

Karan's presence in her phone was becoming addictive, more than any mind-numbing game of bubble-pop or self-congratulatory social media post could ever be. She loved seeing his name light up her phone screen. She felt a thrill each time she watched the ellipses signifying that he was typing out another text to her appear on the screen.

They messaged each other first thing in the morning and punctuated each day with a goodnight text. In between, there was an endless stream of chatter that flowed effortlessly between them like a river, at times shallow and silly, at other points as deep as the sea. He liked to talk and it helped that he was a master conversationalist. She found everything he had to say enthralling, whether it was some musing that crossed his mind during the workday or a late-night confession. He was clever, first and foremost. It was as entertaining as it was sexy. And yes, Milli could admit to herself that she found a man whose face she had never seen very, very sexy.

She found his diction and the careful way in which he expressed his thoughts very attractive and unlike anyone else she had ever spoken to in her life. Most of her friends were constantly tired, unwilling to entertain philosophy in favour of catching a few more minutes of sleep in between shifts. Her mother was incoherent. Her brother was no more. Rahull was not the man she could seek comfort in. But Karan was stimulating and Milli found herself starving for him. She wondered if she would ever get her fill of his thoughts. He had so many of them, and she had been craving something new for so long.

He was as good a listener as he was a texter, as willing to taste someone else's life as he was to give her a bite of his own thoughts. He was courteous; he didn't press when Milli would rather skirt around the issues in her life than confess her suffering to him. But he was all ears when she opened up. Although she had an inkling that he was a busy man, he seemed to be fully focused on her problems when she dared to confess them. Once they spoke about the empty hole her brother had left in her chest when he had died so senselessly in a war she was growing to hate. Another time it was the gnawing acid in the pit of her stomach that grew every time her mother took a swig from a bottle or popped a pill when she thought Milli wasn't looking. Karan listened. He worried for her. He offered advice only when she asked. And it was always measured, seeming to come out of experience.

Are you sure you're only twenty-eight? She would ask every time he spoke from the heart, relaying his thoughts to her.

I may be an old soul, but in this lifetime, I am only twenty-eight. I feel as though I've lived a million years sometimes, he confessed one night, and she could feel the exhaustion seeping into the text message he sent. She wasn't sure what to say in response, then realized she could say anything.

If you turned me inside out, I'd be an old woman, she said. *Sometimes, I think it shows. I've been falling for so long, there's no spring to my step any longer. I'm just a body waiting to hit rock bottom.*

Then we're falling together, he sent in one text. And, after a minute, *then we're made for each other.*

He meant what he said in both messages but wasn't sure which one rang more true.

Yes, she had responded to both. She wasn't sure which one she believed more, either. She hadn't believed in much for a long time. But she was beginning to believe in Karan.

When she would rather bear the weight of his burdens than speak about herself anymore, he would close the book on her stress and allow her a glimpse into his own. He would prattle on about a problem he was facing at work or how much he hated the distance that had sprung up between him and the rest of his family ever since his father had moved to Scotland to handle their company's expanding grip on the European market. Karan was quickly becoming both a best friend and a romantic interest for Milli with each passing day.

It was partly an escapist fantasy she indulged in with every glance at her phone. She enjoyed burying herself in his thoughts instead of the worried, well-worn patterns of her own mind. He would text in paragraphs with impeccable grammar and the occasional word she would have to pull up her Miriam Webster app just to understand. There was no chatspeak to be seen. He was well educated, although he confessed he was mostly self-taught.

I did a lot of correspondence schooling, and spent a lot more time buried in my studies than playing in the playground with friends.

That was the only explanation he had offered for a lot of his past. There were mentions of home-schooling and spending most of his time around adults, even as a small child. Whether that was because of his father's European ventures or due to some other reason, Milli couldn't say. He would make a joke and deflect whatever hurt he still felt about that particular time in his life. Milli could tell he was practised at finding the humour in a dark situation. And that he had been lonely, like she had been, for most of his life. She liked him all the more for it.

I never had many friends, even when I was little, Milli confessed. *Other kids didn't understand me and I never made the effort to get to know them either. My brother and I lived in our own little world and learned how to shelter each other from the storms around us. It didn't leave much room for other people.*

My sister was the social butterfly of the family, he responded. *And I was the little worker bee. But we were close in our own way, despite our differences. She did the things I couldn't and kept me from feeling like I was missing out. I kept her grounded when she was in danger of flying too far from the nest too soon. My family and I were so close growing up, like cogs functioning in the same machine. It was when we weren't living in the same place that things begin to fall out of sync.*

For all he revealed, there was still so much he held back. He was willing to talk about the work he did, although he wouldn't reveal the name of the company his family owned or the specific things he handled; only that they were boring, complicated and completely uninteresting to most people who weren't already familiar with the ins and outs of their industry. He was willing to talk about his family, but not to show her his face. She knew more about him than almost anybody else, but she didn't even know his last name. He was, essentially, an enigma.

He thwarted her Googling at every turn, and although it disappointed her, she understood him. *When you've had as much practice at deflection as I have, it's second nature,* he confessed once, an apology she accepted without much question. Karan was so generous with so much, it made sense that he would hold back on the precious things, the things that mattered most to him. But little by little, his walls were coming down. Piece by piece, she was putting him together. And she liked what she saw of who he really was.

Could she have a crush on a man she had only exchanged text messages with? Could she love him? She had never been in a situation like this before. She had never even heard of a situation like this. Searches for online, long-distance relationships had revealed stories of sweethearts in different continents, semesters abroad and months spent Skyping. It covered protocol for a temporary separation between lovers who had spent time in each other's arms. It did not cover falling in love with a man you had never met.

Still, Milli guarded her heart. It was too easy to let him have all of her when she hadn't had more than a taste of who he really was. And, as she tried to remind herself, there was no real way of knowing if he was who he said he was. Perhaps he was a sociopath inventing a world of his own fantasy and testing it out on a susceptible girl he had met on a dating site. But somehow, she didn't think so. There was something guileless and truthful about Karan. And although it might sound naïve, Milli felt as though their connection ran deeper than the power of technology; they were connected at heart. They were friends, at the very least, and Milli was beginning to think that Karan was the truest friend she had ever had.

They laughed about one of the few things it seemed they had in common, despite having grown up on two very different sides of the same town: a love for golgappa water from the cheapest, shadiest looking food carts in the worst parts of town. Milli's mother would bring her up a big styrofoam cup full of the spicy treat on her way back from late shifts at the hospital, always passed along with an futile lecture on sharing with her brother. Her mother knew she wouldn't but she didn't seem to mind. It was one of the things she would do to make Milli feel special, back when she was still interested in making Milli feel anything other than guilty.

My father would come back from business trips from the Chandigarh airport. At first, he would bring gifts that were too fine for me to appreciate — collector's items, things from far-off lands to store away for later when I was less clumsy and my tastes more refined like his were. But he soon realized I didn't care for those things, that he was wasting his money. My father is an efficient man. He hates waste. He'd swing by an old convenience store on his way to our home and get me tacky keychains, glittering snow globes that would break within the week. But the smile on my face was worth it for him. Eventually, he'd bring home a treat, some sweets from the airport or fried street food, something to balance all the healthy food my mother insisted I stuff myself with. What really stuck though, was the golgappa from a spot not five minutes from the airport. I started to associate the treat with the joy of having him home again. In time, I lost my taste for junk food and appreciated my mother's home-cooked meals but I still order golgappa from time to time, just to feel the way I used to feel. The original stand my father used to frequent had been closed for years, but it's easy to find good golgappa nearly anywhere.

Her phone buzzed again a moment later.

Sorry for the novel. Before you, I never used to reminisce like this about anything or anyone.

She tapped out a response as quickly as her fingers would let her.

Before you, I never used to remember the past so sweetly. But you make my present feel kinder and it doesn't hurt as much to think about the past.

It didn't hurt her anymore to think about the future, either, but she wasn't ready to confess to Karan that her dreams of the future now lay with him. She couldn't pinpoint exactly when it was that she had started to feel this way about him. She wasn't sure whether it was okay for her to feel the way she did about him or whether he felt the same way. But she could see the future more clearly than she had ever been able to in her life, even though it was all fantasy and as thin as air. When she closed her eyes, she could even feel his hand in hers.

At that moment her phone vibrated and she saw Karan's name on her screen. She was a little surprised when she read the text message. It wasn't as though it was unwelcomed, but she generally expected philosophical lines of inquiry or commentary on the magic of Paris from him. But late at night, she could feel the champagne buzz in his tone as he wandered along the Seine.

If your hand were in mine right now, I'd have the world at my feet. What I wouldn't do to kiss you right here under the Parisian sky, still pink with lights even at this late hour.

She had always known he was a poet, but sometimes his way with words made her dizzy. Still, something about the night, the Chandigarh sky with so many stars in comparison to Paris' glowing atmosphere, set something alight in her. With Karan so honest, she wanted to be honest in response.

What I wouldn't give to be there, she replied. *To feel your lips against mine, your body pressing close to mine, protecting me from the cool of the night and the glances of the tourists around us.*

And wouldn't they be jealous of us? Lovers in the Parisian night? They'd want to stare, in anger, in jealousy, in something more. I'd have

to hide you away under what little cover of darkness the night here
provides and find a more private place for us.

Milli was definitely blushing now if she hadn't been before.
There was something commanding in the lines of his poetry;
he seemed as confident as a man who knew all too well what he
wanted and how to gain it for himself. And it seemed to Milli that
he wanted her, entirely, and alone. What would he do then, she
wondered, if he had her, like it seemed he had everything else he
wanted in this world? There was only one way to find out. But,
before Milli could ask him another text from Karan popped up on
her screen.

What would I do? he sent a text again. For a moment, that
seemed to be it.

Then the ellipses appeared on Milli's screen and stayed that
way for quite some time.

When his next message came, Milli felt as though by reading
it she was transcending the distance that life had put upon them.
She felt as though she were really there in his arms with the river
flowing by them and the night chilly around them like a thin
blanket. Lovers by a riverbed. What a place to be.

My dear, if you were here with me in Paris, I wouldn't be alone by the
river sipping champagne and pondering whether or not fate possessed
an ounce of mercy, he told her frankly. *If you were here I'd know the*
universe was merciful and loving without a hint of malice within it.
How could it be anything but sweet, with you in this world and so close
to me? If you were here, it would be a different story.

You deserve better than clandestine kisses by the river in the
Parisian night. You deserve the full opulence of the morning, the crisp
white sheets and a whole weekend with nowhere to be but in bed with
me. You deserve strawberries and champagne out of the glass, not the
bottle. You deserve wine and roses and the slow, lingering sort of kisses

that last hours. The sort of kisses that have your body buzzing and your soul on fire even before a stitch of clothing is removed.

Milli sat dumbfounded, looking at the words on her phone. No one had spoken to her like this before. Not with so much frankness and never with so much romance in their heart. Karan spoke as if Milli were precious and incredible, the sort of woman to be seduced by pulling all the stops, to be showered with gifts and handled as delicately as if she were some intricate bit of luxury instead of a callous-handed girl from the country. If he spoke this way to all the girls...well, well, he would probably have been married years ago. No girl in her right mind would ever let go of a man like him.

Which might mean, Milli realized, that he just liked her that much. And that was even more troubling in its own way. Being the object of that much affection, pure and seemingly without any alternate agenda, was something Milli had never considered might happen to her. She was used to Rahull's obsession and her mother's total dependence upon her. But neither of those things could be considered to be love. She was worried that love was what this might be.

The thought frightened her, but not as much as she thought it would. It just felt natural...like everything else did with Karan. Loving him wasn't an alien a concept to her. It was an instinctual thing. Something she couldn't help. She supposed that was why they called it 'falling' in love. It was so natural, so completely out of your control, like a side effect of gravity and not a choice at all. Still, she supposed that 'falling' hurt less than she had always assumed it would.

Have I scared you off?

No, by all means, continue.

Milli hadn't even realized that she could text so quickly.

If we were in Paris, we'd have to stay at least two weeks. The first week, you'd see little more than the inside of our hotel room. We'd order room service for every meal, live decadently, the kind of way Parisians believe you should live. Good food and good sex.

And wasn't that a fascinating proposition, to live decadently?

And in the second week?

The second week, I'd take you to all the places I've been wandering by myself, but I'd hold your hand instead of just the thought of you on my phone. But back to the first week. Are you going to participate, or is this purely a spectator sport for you? Not that I mind either way, of course.

Milli bit her lip, considering. She had always wanted to be the sort of woman who lived inside her romance novels. She had wanted to be the kind of woman who looked good laying on a bed in a fancy Parisian hotel, eating strawberries and looking at a handsome man with a come-hither look in her eyes. But she had never truly been able to envision herself that way. She was Milli. And that was a good thing when it came to working hard and keeping the people around her alive, but it had never been good when it came to romance. But right now, she was the Milli of Karan's fantasies and dreams and that Milli could certainly try.

The only thing that could pull me away from the view of Paris at night would be you. I'd want you to hold me in your strong arms, to test your strength and see just how bold you really are. I'd want your full attention and I know you'd be the person to give it to me just the way I want it. My dream is a view of the streets at night from our hotel window, you with your arms around me, pressing kisses down my neck. I shiver at the very thought of it, you holding me so closely, touching me, the taste of your lips sweeter than anything any patisserie had to offer.

She stopped herself there, hitting send before she could talk herself out of it. The pleasant twist in her stomach that was part anticipation and part arousal, the hint of dread weighing on her shoulders, made her body feel electric in a way it never had before. How could a man she had never met make her feel this way? That too with just his words. It was as though he could tap directly into her mind and know exactly the right things to say to bring her soul to life. And that fire he sparked in her was catching flame.

Wow was his initial response, but Milli could see the ellipses hinting that around the corner lay a stream of incredible texts that would leave her blushing, gasping, and begging for more. She had always been a romantic at heart, but now there was someone interested in the inner workings of her heart. He seemed to like what he saw there and she liked him.

It was so comfortable to lie in her bed and pretend that he was by her side, whispering these words in her ear when her vision blurred from exhaustion. She could feel the weight of him next to her in bed, could smell his skin, could feel his strong arms surrounding her, holding her tight as she slept. The heat of his body close to hers, the sound of his breath…it was all in her imagination, but it felt so real. Just like the words he messaged to her did.

Now all she could think about, dream about, was meeting him in real life. Any man who could inspire her like that, who could give her so much to dream about while being in another country using only his words, not even his voice, was worth at least grabbing a coffee with. And if it led to the kind of things he was describing, evenings with wine and strawberries, and hotel rooms that they got good use out of, well, Milli certainly wouldn't complain. This kind of a romance came along once in a lifetime. And for people like Milli, sometimes it never came at all. She wouldn't be shy in pursuing it.

A text from Karan buzzed, startling her from sound sleep in the middle of the night. A picture of Charles de Gaulle's domed ceiling. *Au Revoir, Paris!* the text read.

Milli meant to say, *hope your trip was great. Thanks for showing me Paris.*

What she sent instead was, *I might be falling for you*. However, before her phone could buzz with Karan's response, Milli was asleep, dreaming of Karan and nothing else. She would have time to worry tomorrow about whatever she had said tonight. Besides, she was pretty sure that Karan was falling for her, too.

SIX

Milli wasn't heartbroken yet. She was, however, confused and bewildered. After such a lovely few days, the radio silence from Karan's end since his leaving Paris made her feel used and abandoned. She had opened her heart to him and he hadn't seen fit to respond. Trying not to seem desperate, she messaged him a few times on WhatsApp; a simple, *How are you? Hope your day is good! :)* which got no response. She even contacted him on Clickrr, though his profile showed he hadn't been active on the site since before he left Paris. She had kept her eye on the news for reports of a plane crash in France but had seen nothing. He had landed safely. He was somewhere close by. And he wasn't answering Milli's calls.

Milli generally thought of herself as an easy-come easy-go sort of person. She had gotten fairly used to people filtering in and out of her life. She could let Karan go. She told herself this over and over, as she tried to scrub at a particularly difficult bit of baked-on pasta out of a pan. And besides, it was what she deserved for working herself up into such a state, for giving into such sweet daydreams of escaping with Karan and making a new life together. Girls like Milli always got left behind. In a matter of years, she would become her mother, raising a little girl in the house she had grown up in. A lonely child and a lonely mother. No man in sight.

Her phone buzzed, and she buried the hope in her heart before checking it. Holding her heart in check had been the right instinct because it wasn't Karan texting her, it was Rahull, once more.

Just ran into your mother at the supermarket, the text read. *She seemed pretty out of it. What are you doing tonight?*

She rolled her eyes, setting her phone back down on the kitchen counter and picking up the steel wool once more. He hadn't gotten the hint although she had been fairly explicit over the years and he wouldn't get it now. She wasn't interested but he didn't care. He figured he could wait her out until she had exhausted all her options. And perhaps he was right. It was easy enough to stick around when you lived in such close proximity. Maybe one day she would give up and walk to his home. When the pain of being alone exceeded the pain of accepting that this had been her fate all along, she would go to him.

But today was not that day, she told herself, returning to her task with renewed vigour. The pain of Karan's sudden disappearance wouldn't convince her to give up. It tired her to think about how much she missed him. She tried to convince herself that she only missed the fantasy, the attention, and that there was nothing special about this boy in particular. Sometimes she could work hard enough to distract herself to the point where she almost believed her own platitudes.

Her phone buzzed again. Rahull.

What're you doing tonight? Let's go out.

Classic Rahull, knowing he could goad her into replying if he sent her enough messages. He thought he was being persistent; she thought he was being obnoxious. She rubbed her soapy hands against a dish towel and picked up the phone.

nothing

It was their dynamic. He would irritate her until she would retaliate with one-word answers, blocking him at every turn until he would leave her alone. Rahull was the mosquito buzzing in her ear but it wouldn't do well to brush him off. He would just come back later and bite again.

You wanna go out tonight?

She huffed a laugh, drying the pan she had been scrubbing with her dish towel.

no

His response came back quicker than she had expected.

Just thought I'd offer. Your mom seemed pretty out of it when I saw her. Doubt it'll get better.

Dinner and a movie. There's a drive-in theatre festival on that you might like.

Just think about it, Milli. Neither of us are getting any younger.

And your mom isn't getting any better.

And there it was – the root of the issue. The dragon guarding the castle, keeping Milli trapped in her tower. Not her mother but her mother's addiction. All the fantasizing about Karan in Paris or a world into which she could escape and be free did her no good. The world she was leaving behind when she closed her eyes was a dangerous one with broken sinks and crumbling houses. Her mother was too sick to be left on her own.

But maybe Milli could escape for one night. As much as she hated it, the alternative Rahull offered her was better than sitting around the house, scrubbing pans and getting older, trying to make certain her mother didn't take too much of anything or destroy anything besides her own body. She had no friends with whom she could drink coffee and chat the night away. She held a lone vigil over her mother. It might be nice to let her guard down for one night, even if it was with Rahull.

The romantic part of Milli's soul held her back. It longed for pain au chocolat with Karan under the Parisian stars. What if he came back for her? No one ever had before, but Karan was like no one she had ever met. She had let herself fall thinking he might be an exception and it was hard to shake that feeling despite the testimonial of her silent phone staring her in the face.

Milli prided herself on being a pragmatist and a realist. If evidence showed that men didn't come back, men wouldn't come back. Not even incredible men like Karan. She sighed, wiping her hands dry once more. She hesitated with the message she sent to Rahull, deleting and retyping it over and over before finally hitting send.

sure, it read, *why not?*

———•———

It certainly wasn't a picnic under the Eiffel Tower. Instead, it was a cramped booth at the dirty restaurant that smelled of frying grease and motor exhaust. It was dirty floors and the tired face behind the counter of a girl she had gone to secondary school with who rarely spoke and never smiled. It was boring pav bhaji, the lacklustre cousin of a spicy meal, and the ire she felt as Rahull kept trying to steal from her plate when he had gulped down his own meal in five minutes. It was uncomfortable and awkward, a silence that Milli would have been content to continue forever, interrupted at increasingly desperate intervals by Rahull's incessant chatter. The conversation was almost entirely about himself, his promotion at the factory, the work he was doing renovating his parents' old place.

It was hard for her to remember what Rahull looked like anymore, even with him sitting right in front of her. So many years of overlooking him made it hard to keep a clear picture of his face in her mind. She could tick off a list of characteristics: large and burly, skin stained red from work, prone to sweating through his shirts, his dirty hair greying at the temples, thinning at the crown. Despite knowing him most of her life, she couldn't recall the colour of his eyes. She darted a glance up at him to check. Light brown, she realized, and forgot again the next moment.

A cautious smile spread over his lips when her gaze met his. He paused mid-sentence to see if she had something to say. The smile faded almost immediately when she looked back down at her plate. He fell back into his monologue after a moment, not to be discouraged. Milli sank into her own thoughts.

If Milli were listening more closely, she would have heard the way he was setting himself up for her, like a bill of goods for her to peruse and find worthy. But she found herself unable to focus what he said. His words lulled her, his voice a dull monotonous tune playing in the background of the monochrome diner. Perhaps it was the tiredness she felt or the way his chatter wore her down further. Perhaps it was the worry let go, having left her mother home alone she was unable to let go. But she couldn't even muster up a smile at the weak jokes he made or nod along as he spoke.

'Milli? Milli?' he asked her, waving a hand in front of her face. 'Hey? Milli!'

'What? Oh, sure,' she responded without bothering to figure out what he had asked her, pushing her plate towards him.

He scowled, but it didn't stop him from taking the last few bites of her pav bhaji. She was about to apologize, aware that she had crossed a line of rudeness she might not have if she'd slept longer than a wink within the past month. But before she could say anything, her phone buzzed. She swore under her breath.

'Is that your mom?' he asked, leaning in. 'Is everything alright?'

She hummed under her breath, fishing her phone out of her purse. She knew it had been a mistake to leave her mother alone but she hadn't thought there would be an emergency so early into the night. She had planned to be back home by 10 p.m., before her mother's witching hour when the real trouble started to occur. It was only 8.12 p.m.

The text only read: *I'm sorry for my absence.*

It took her longer than it should have to realize that it wasn't from her mother. It was from Karan.

Her heart leapt. Light and colour filled the hollow cavity in her chest, expanding across her vision. Suddenly the dim, dirty restaurant looked almost lovely. The world looked a little softer, a little better. All because Karan was back in it.

Are you okay? I was worried, she shot off, knowing she sounded a little desperate and knowing Karan wouldn't care. It was honest, after all, and that was what he wanted from her.

'Who is that, Milli?' Rahull asked, unable to keep the petulant note out of his voice.

'It was – oh, it was my mom,' Milli replied, unwilling to risk his wrath by telling him the truth. Rahull's temper had mellowed a little in recent years, but he was still the kind of country boy who could get angry at the drop of a hat.

'She okay?'

Not entirely okay. It's a long story and one for another day. I've missed you terribly.

Karan missed her? The room felt light and buzzed with possibility. Karan hadn't left her after all. He had wanted to be with her, but something had stopped him from doing so. A smile spread across her face, not entirely of her own volition. Even as she worried for him, she was happy for them. The possibility of *KaranandMilli* still existed for them. Her world felt surreal. Like something she had dreamed up.

Rahull's scowl deepened but Milli didn't notice.

'Well, I suppose from the look on your face, your mother is doing great,' he huffed. He gestured to the waitress, who brought the check. He pulled a few notes out of his overstuffed wallet and set them on the table.

'Nuh-uh. I'm paying my half,' Milli said, pulling some money out of her wallet and pushing a few of his back towards him.

'Milli, just let me get it.'

'I said I've got my half,' she insisted.

But he wouldn't budge. 'And I'm saying that's completely unnecessary,' he shoved her money back towards her. 'If we don't get a move on, we're going to be late for the film.'

'Well then, I suppose you'd better take your money back if you don't want to be late,' she crossed her arms in front of her chest. If she paid her half, he would understand that this was not a date. Which was probably why he was so intent on paying: he wanted it to be a date.

'Quit being so stubborn,' he hissed, 'you're making a scene.'

'I'm paying my half,' she insisted, 'if you don't want to take your money back, I suppose that waitress is just going to get a hell of a tip.'

'I suppose she will,' he grumbled. 'You want to come on then or are you going to insist on driving yourself separately to the movie, as well, in the name of feminism or whatever it is that's making you so uppity these days?'

Mili bristled with indignation. *His name is Karan*, she thought to herself, but shrugged, slinging her purse on and walking past Rahull with a scowl. She knew that letting him drive was a mistake. She was forced to go wherever he wanted as long as he was behind the wheel. He let the door to the diner slam shut but closed the door of his car with a little less force. Either he was trying to calm down or he was more invested in his own property than other people's. She fished her phone out of her purse, tapping out a message to Karan as Rahull's diesel engine roared to life.

I think I missed you more.

Not possible. I've never been more lonely in my life than I was in these past few weeks without you. Or maybe I've always been this lonely but with you I forgot how bad it could feel. I'm glad I'm finally able to reach out to you.

I thought you were gone without a word, she told him. *It made my loneliness feel stronger than it did before you came along.*

Tears welled in her eyes as the feeling of relief washed over her, cleansing the worry, grief and anger she had felt when she thought he had left her. He hadn't left her at all. He still saw something worth pursuing in her. The very thought amazed her. It was so different from anything she had ever known.

'Your mother again? She sure is chatty tonight,' Rahull scowled, turning into the drive-in movie theatre with a little more force than required. Milli had always loved the outdoor theatre, listening to the hum of tree frogs as she sat in the back of someone's car, watching the movie projected on a large screen in the open air. But she couldn't help but dread spending the duration of the movie sitting next to Rahull. Milli shrugged. Karan's text lit up her screen and her smile lit up her face.

Then I'll try not to leave you again.

Rahull pulled up at the venue. Outside, a pay-station was set up, and he rolled down his window to buy their tickets. The guy at the counter must have been a friend of his, because his demeanour went from aggressive to easy-going within a few seconds. It relieved Milli to see the tightness in his shoulders loosen. Even if he was still simmering under the surface, at least he wouldn't snap at her while his pals were watching. He laughed about something Milli couldn't hear, pressing a few bills into the attendant's hand before maneuvering the car into the parking lot.

There were several other cars parked in the lot. Rahull parked in a way that allowed the car to face the movie screen, dialling his car radio to the station where the sound from the movie would play and cranking the volume loud enough that it washed over Milli in a tidal wave of sound, making her wince.

'I got supplies.' Rahull grunted, extracting a mess of quilts from the back of his car. An empty bottle of coke rolled off the seat and onto the floor. 'Blankets, some soft drinks and chips if you want.'

'I can get my own snacks,' she told him.

'Be as stubborn as you want but it seems a foolish thing to pay theatre rates for stale popcorn when you could be eating these chips for free,' the smile that spread across his face was a lawyer's smile, all bright and false. It seemed his temper had subsided for now, but it was clear the fury still lingered under the surface. 'You suit yourself though, Milli Bajwa. You just keep doing what you've always done.'

His keen assessment of her made Milli a little uncomfortable. She did feel a small amount of guilt for letting Rahull drag her out and then ignoring him all night. But she hadn't known that Karan would ever contact her again. And it wasn't as though Rahull had been particularly kind to her the whole evening. She wondered what had become of the boy she had known since they were toddlers, bringing her daisies from the field and being satisfied with only holding her hand. She couldn't understand his resentment or why she seemed to be the source of it.

She settled into the seat, watching the previews. They were always the best part. When Rahull handed her the chips, she accepted them without looking at him. She heard the cracking of two soda cans opening beside her.

'They're still cold,' Rahull offered.

'Thanks,' she took one from him with a smile, then turned back to the screen. It unnerved her to feel Rahull's eyes still on her. It was as though he wasn't interested in watching the movie at all.

They sat in silence through the start of the film. A few times she felt as though Rahull might say something. It seemed as though he was gearing up to speak. But he kept silent well through the first fifteen minutes. Milli ignored her cell phone the first couple of times it buzzed, resolving to enjoy the film and be a good guest. Rahull was being hospitable. The least she could do was be courteous in response.

But as Rahull shifted closer to her in a way he imagined was subtle, the car got more and more claustrophobic for Milli. She inched away trying not to be very obvious about her revulsion. She slid up along the seat casually like she was trying to find a more comfortable position. Rahull followed suit and squeezed himself beside her. Now she could feel his hot breath on her averted face. Only then did she realize that she was almost halfway out of the car but Rahull wasn't letting up. It was only when Milli was wedged against the door with no more room left that she realized he was very close to her face and she had no way of evading his advances other than vaulting out of the car.

Landing on the pavement was a little rougher than she had expected. The gravel that pressed into her legs stung. She hoped that maybe she had misunderstood the situation and that Rahull would be laughing hard, teasing her about what a fool she had been for launching herself out of the car for no reason. But even in the darkness, Rahull's face was grave.

'If you didn't wanna kiss me you shouldn't have come out tonight, Milli. I'm a reasonable man. I wouldn't have caused any trouble. But you've been leading me on all night and I don't appreciate it.' He tossed her purse out of his car. She caught it, still numb with shock.

'You can find your own ride home. Maybe with that boyfriend you've been texting all night or your pill-popping mother. I don't care,' he hissed. With that he climbed into the car, slamming the door shut and starting the engine with a roar. He drove out of the parking lot, not bothering to wave to his friend at the entrance as he tore back down the road.

Milli swore and swore again. Thankfully, her home was a only little over two kilometres away. Could she risk walking it? She knew it had been a bad idea to let Rahull drive but she hadn't realized he would abandon her alone.

With no cabs or autos available in this area, she knew that her only option was to walk. She stood, up and dusted herself off. There was probably someone in the lot who knew her and would probably give her a ride home but her pride wouldn't allow her to interrupt their night because she had been foolish. So she set off, knowing that if she left right that second she would be able to make it home in a little under an hour. It was only 9 pm. At this time, with people still out and the roads still busy, she would be fine. She waved to the man at the front as she turned in the same direction that Rahull's headlights had disappeared.

The moon was bright overhead, clear enough for her to see most of the obstacles on her path. She could hear cars coming up behind her long before they would pose any threat to her. The weather was warm and pleasant enough. Chandigarh heat was always a little steamy and it might leave her sweating by the time she got home, but it was no different from running around catching fireflies as a little kid. It was almost a pleasant exertion. The one thing she missed was company.

It seemed only natural, considering they had been chatting all night, that Karan would be the one she would call. She wanted to hear somebody's voice as she trudged down the road. And if she was being honest, which she tried to be for Karan's sake, his voice was the only one she wanted to hear.

She was surprised at how quickly he answered her call. It was as though he was waiting by the phone.

'Hey,' she said, a little awkward and breathless, 'I just wanted to hear your voice.'

'I wanted to hear yours too, if I'm being honest,' there was a little smile in his voice. His voice was deeper than she had imagined. A little hoarse, as though he had just been woken up. There was a ring of familiarity to it that she hadn't expected, like remembering a snippet of a dream long after you woke up the next day.

'Did I wake you?' she asked, suddenly nervous.

'No, no, I've been up for a while,' he reassured her. There was a loud beep from his end of the line, and he bit off a swear. 'Really. I'm glad you called. I'm nearly crawling out of my skin with boredom here.'

'Where are you? And what's that beeping?' Milli asked, skipping over a storm sewer and onto the rumble strip of the highway.

'I – nothing. It's the TV. Don't ask,' he stumbled as though the question had caught him off-guard.

'I won't ask,' she said. Wherever he was, it couldn't be more worrying than walking alone on the side of a highway in rural Chandigarh. If she couldn't ask him where he was, he couldn't ask her. Fair was fair.

'So, how's your night been so far?' he asked. She let out a loud groan.

'Don't ask,' she insisted as he laughed. 'I've got a long walk home and a bunch of chores waiting for me when I get there. It sounds like neither of us are having a great night.'

'Mine got better once you called,' he told her. And if Milli blushed, there was no one there to see it in the darkness.

They talked all night until a pale sliver of sunlight broke across the horizon. Under the hazy night full of bright stars, they talked softly. Milli felt as though Karan's hand were in hers, as though he were along for this journey with her physically instead of just a voice on the phone. More than once Karan yawned, his voice hoarse, his thoughts tired and rambling. Milli insisted each time that he go to sleep. But he retorted that he had been resting for far too long already. 'Besides, talking to you is much better than anything I'd dream about tonight.'

And what was Milli supposed to say to that? She felt the stars glowing brighter around her every time he spoke. She was afraid that she was falling too fast and afraid that he wouldn't fall fast enough to catch her. She wanted to say something vitally important, something amazing that would bring him to his knees. She wanted to behave like a heroine from one of the pulp novels she loved. But she couldn't and she didn't. What she did end up saying was, 'I can see my house from here.'

'Well, I suppose I should let you get back to the pile of chores you mentioned.'

'I'll only let you hang up on me if you promise to get some sleep,' she smiled. She slipped off her shoes in the yard so that she could slip into the house undetected. The feeling of fresh dew in the grass against her bare skin felt as sweet as Karan's voice in her ear.

'It won't be hard for me to fall asleep. But I was glad to have someone keeping me company tonight.'

'Have a good night,' she whispered, tiptoeing across the porch.

'You too,' he responded. And with a click, he was gone. Milli sighed. Easing open the front door, she saw her mother asleep on the couch. The world had not ended in her one night of absence. Climbing into bed, images of the night swam before her eyes. It may have started off rough but it hadn't been a total waste. She had her momentary escape after all.

SEVEN

The warm light of the library blurred before Karan's eyes as pain jolted through his body. He leaned harder on his crutches hoping that they would continue to support his weight and not give way. He felt so off balance, both physically and mentally. One wrong move might send him tumbling down the floor, unable to get up. He could only hope Amit would find him in time, if that were to happen. He was playing a dangerous game, but danger was preferable to the endless boredom of lying in bed, waiting to heal.

Pills numbed his pain a little but they could not numb his frustration. The heartbreak. The fear. The only relief he could think of from the tumultuous feelings inside of him was to lose himself in someone else's story, one with a guaranteed happy ending and plenty of joyous moments along the way. Escaping into a romance novel where he could imagine someone by his side had been his way, of leaving the painful world behind.

But nothing in his library seemed to do the trick. One book was too boring, the next was too sad. One contained a love scene that made him cringe with vicarious embarrassment. Another was peppered with jokes that fell flat. All the stories that used to make him smile left him feeling bereft and abandoned. Not even his favourite books could help him remember the joy he once felt flipping through their pages. Nothing felt quite right. Nothing felt as good as what he and Milli had.

But what could he tell Milli? What could he say to her that wouldn't send her running for the hills as soon as she found out who he truly was? Sad, crippled, lonely, wasting away in the house that had once been his haven. Would she panic? Or worse, pity him? What would she think when she realized she was dreaming of a future with a broken man?

He leaned his head against the spines of the books as another blast of pain washed over him, drowning him in it. Movement was difficult. Staying still was even harder. His own body was his personal hell. There was no release. No escape from the torment his own bones put him through. What he wouldn't give to sleep for months and wake up with a healed body and Milli by his side. But that couldn't happen.

As his vision cleared, he realized he was leaning on the spine of one of the first books he had published. A tome of emotional poetry written during a time in his life when he thought the world couldn't get any darker. *Foolish boy*, he thought now, remembering the boy he had once been, *did you really think that your life would get easier? Did you really have that much hope?*

He flipped open the book, scanning the page numbers until he alighted on a poem that summed up the way he was feeling now. He was just a boy when it was written, forced head-first into adulthood by a surgery most men would never suffer through. The words still rang true to him, it amazed him how little it had changed in ten years.

Alone Again
Four o'clock in the morning
Afraid to open my eyes
Another day of grief
A day of fear
I try to justify this pain
All of this guilt before my eyes

Another day of confusion
A day of wondering
All this pain that I feel
And all this anger, is it going to stay?
Ten o'clock in the evening
Afraid of the nightmares
Again my breathing stops
All I can do is stare into the night
What is it that causes this feeling?
Another night of crying
A night of hiding
Alone once again
My heart feels empty
And I can't shed another tear
Another day wasted on insecurity
A day of apprehension.
Is this ever going to end?

Nothing had changed. If anything, he was more alone than ever before. He had hoped his luck would change, and for a few years, it seemed like that it had. One moment he had it all and lost it all the next. Now, he was surrounded by people who couldn't or wouldn't understand what he was going through.

But it was partially his own fault, wasn't it? For years, he had sought only the company of beautiful, shallow people who disappeared the moment things turned grim. He closed himself to any hope of being loved or saved by those who might be willing to understand him. He suffered in silence, trapped in the chambers of the house he once loved. Still wondering, *is this ever going to end?*

Unstable on his crutches, wobbling like a colt on new legs, he made his way into the living room. The sight of his parents' portrait on the wall made his heart sting. Seeing them holding his squirming sister, his own young face staring back at him reminded him of what a sanctuary of happiness this house had once been. But it had not been that way for many years now.

He took it all in, wondering at the state of the darkened room, so removed from its former glory. The couches where he and his sister hid from Amit on rainy afternoons, playing their own game of hide-and-seek to the exasperation of the old man. The bar where his parents entertained their friends late into the evening, filling their massive home with life and laughter. This was the room where he had taken his first steps as a child, and now, as a fully-grown man, he could barely walk at all. His home was empty now with only Karan left to haunt the corridors like a ghost.

Tucked under the bar was a bottle of scotch his father had sent to him last year as a celebration of the many successes they had had that year with their business. At that time, Karan hadn't touched it, saving it for a rainy day and pushing it to the back of his liquor cabinet. Scotch was bitter and intense, nothing Karan ever wanted to consume. He would toast with his employees and friends every once in a while and had schooled himself not to wince as the drink burned its way through his body. But he had never liked the taste.

Still, he thought, as he opened the bottle, he didn't have to love the taste for it to numb the pain.

———•———

The scotch didn't taste like a celebration. It didn't feel like a party as it made its way through his veins, humming electric blue through his thoughts and clouding his mind. There was no joy in its flavour, no victory in the way it burned down his throat. But it was doing the trick. He stared deeply into the bottle as though he could divine an answer to his situation.

He finished almost a quarter of the bottle. Everything around him was a haze, his thoughts swimming through his mind as slowly as if they were moving through molasses. The mixture of medication and scotch in his body made everything feel smaller, insignificant, like he was floating far above his body and all hell was below him. He smiled grimly at the irony of his escape. He took another sip chasing the numbing sensation. Perhaps, at the end of it, he would escape his hell and find heaven.

He didn't notice when Amit came into the room, a quiet observer as he often was. Amit lingered at the doorframe for only a moment, assessing the situation with his keen eyes which softened with heartbreak as he understood, watching Karan grimace with each sip of scotch. He went to his ward, settling at the bar stool next to him and sliding the bottle away.

'I thought you hated scotch,' Amit wondered aloud, breaking the silence. Karan smirked, resting his head heavily against the bar and staring up at Amit. His careless movements couldn't hide the tears welling in his eyes.

'On occasions like this, poison is preferable. Scotch tastes like poison but it's too weak to kill me,' he told Amit, his hoarse voice barely a whisper. Amit nodded sagely, taking a pull from the bottle before capping it and tucking it back into the liquor cabinet.

'Do you want to die?' he asked Karan, without blame or judgement colouring his voice. The kindness was almost too much for Karan to bear.

He choked on his words, trying to think of the right thing to say. The haze of the alcohol numbed his wit and his tongue was slow to explain to Amit exactly what it was he needed. 'The pain I feel is unbearable, but being away from Milli might be a fate worse than death. I want to be with her but my suffering is so great.'

The simplest explanation was one too difficult to say out loud. *I don't know.* But Amit seemed to understand anyway. He rested a caring, fatherly hand on the nape of Karan's neck, rubbing comforting circles into the exposed skin at his collar. It made Karan feel like a little boy again, protected. His tears flowed openly now.

'I'm neither dead nor alive,' Karan confessed, closing his eyes against the onslaught of pain he felt not in his legs, but in his heart, as he admitted the truth. 'I'm in purgatory, until I either die and go to heaven, or live and go to Milli. Either way, I'll be freed from my suffering.'

Amit's response was pragmatic, his voice strong in Karan's ear. It was all the support that Karan needed to lean on as he struggled through this world of fear and pain. 'You've always spoken of hope, of life, of making your heaven here, in the life you've been given. Karan, my friend, have you lost the zeal to make it happen?'

Something in his words shook Karan to his core, reminding him of why he continued to struggle. It wasn't for his family and it wasn't for Milli. Sure, his love for them was strong, but what was stronger was his love for life. Only he could bring himself to life and keep it there. Even through his misery and pain, he had to live, for his own sake and not for the sake of everyone around him. Amit reminded him that he need to keep fighting. Life is too precious a gift to waste. A world with laughter and fast cars, good food and better people was one worth fighting for. Karan had to remember that this temporary hell came with a promised heaven on the other side.

Finally, he spoke, his voice weak with tears and gratitude. His smile was weak through the pain he felt, but still evident on his face, 'I thought I had lost my zeal, Amit. I didn't know where I'd left it or how to bring it back into my soul. I tried to find my hope at the bottom of this bottle. But you've reminded me that it's been within me all along. I just need to hold on to it.'

Amit nodded encouragingly, with a faint smile on his face.

Karan's face turned dark once more as another spasm of pain shot through him. 'But sometimes, it hurts so much, I can feel everything slipping through my grasp,' he cried, 'and I don't know what to do.'

Wordlessly Amit took Karan in his arms, the way he had when Karan was a boy and too afraid of looking weak to cry in front of his family. He hadn't wanted to scare them with his uncertainties about his surgeries but Amit took it all in and comforted him in a way he couldn't ask anyone else to do. That was Amit's job: supporting them all so easily that they didn't realize how many of their burdens they placed on him.

Amit did now what he had done for years. He held Karan up, running a soothing hand through Karan's hair. 'If the pain and the weight of it is too much to bear,' he told Karan, 'let me bear your burdens for a while. It's what I'm here for. I'll always be here for you.'

And Karan, for the first time since his accident, felt safe enough to completely let go. He dissolved, letting all his fears and the horror he felt go as he sank into Amit's arms, heavy and heaving with sobs. How grateful he felt in that moment to be there with someone, to be understood, to be supported and held until he could hold himself up once more. How grateful he was, in this sea of loneliness and pain, to have a friend who could be there for him. In all his agony and tears, he felt for the first time that he might survive this.

'I want to sleep,' he gasped out finally, though his body was wracked with sobs. Amit simply nodded, running a soothing hand across Karan's shoulders as he helped support his weight. They moved slowly together through the hall, resting when the pain from Karan's hips grew too much to bear, until they found themselves at Karan's bedroom door once again. Amit gently lowered Karan back onto the bed, soothing the hair away from his brow, the way he had done when Karan was sick as a child. The gesture was as familiar and comforting as anything Karan knew and through the haze of his mind, he registered the command to sleep. His body obeyed.

'Amit,' he murmured as he drifted off, exhausted but somehow feeling stronger than he had been in weeks, 'you are my truest friend.'

Through the haze of exhaustion, he thought he heard Amit's reply, 'and you are mine,' before the door closed and he lost himself to sleep.

———————◆———————

Since he had left the hospital and returned home, Milli was quickly becoming Karan's entire world. It was because she held the last vestiges of normalcy in her grasp. When he talked with her or texted her, she made him feel whole and strong. She made him feel like he was still handsome and interesting, capable and mysterious. In reality, the mystery he carried with him would make Milli balk, he was sure. The only mystery in his life was when his hips would finally give out and what horrible fate would befall him next. But with Milli, he could be himself – the person he was beyond the home health nurse and doctor's orders. He was a painter again, a poet, a chef. Only with Milli could he exist the way he wanted to exist.

The existence he wanted for himself did not include bed rest. He thought that the cruellest trick the world had ever played on him was damning him with the disease that forced him to have multiple surgeries. But it seemed that the universe had further miseries in store for him. Milli was his only escape.

And Milli wanted to escape to him. That was what hurt more than the pervasive ache in his hips or his scars from the wreck. That was what he couldn't allow. She would ask in a careful way if he might be interested in meeting up, if she could get him coffee or buy him dinner. He loved her pride, the way she wanted to provide as best she could for him out of her own meagre existence rather than relying on his. He had never met a woman who seemed interested in him just for him and not his money. He hadn't exactly kept his fortune a secret at the start, figuring that she would, like most women, get the measure of it before trying to figure out his interests. But Milli skirted around the subject of his wealth, instead enjoyed talking about the things they both loved.

It made it so easy to love her. She absorbed literature like a sponge and had witty things to say about Neruda and Jonathan Franzen. She could quip about the Brontes with the best of them, and best of all, she was shameless about her love for tawdry pulp romances. Not pretentious, not shallow, not self-absorbed or self-pitying. She truly was like no one Karan had ever met. If he were living in the world of his fantasies, where he was healthy and whole, he might allow himself to fall for Milli.

Instead, he was living in hell.

Bed rest was a damning sentence for a man who hadn't even turned thirty yet. He was full of joie de vivre that his sentence and condition couldn't quite destroy, but it was hard to have a lust for life when one's life was confined to four walls, doctor's visits and home health nurses. It made it all the worse. Sometimes he wished that he would lose his will to fight so that he wouldn't feel so trapped in his own body. His skin felt like a prison containing a man too strong to be crippled this way. The only relief was the escape he made in his own head and on his phone. His escape to Milli.

Still, life in his room wasn't so bad sometimes. Amit did what he could to liven up the place, bringing fresh flowers into the room where he could and making almost constant runs to the public library to satisfy Karan's voracious appetite for literature. He would crack off-colour jokes when Karan was in the mood to laugh and hold his hand in a firm grip when the pain got to be so much that Karan would cry out. He was kind and careful with Karan. Karan would never be able to truly express his gratitude.

An unexpected ally came in the form of Dr Dennis Lox. The man was a force of nature. He was the top doctor in his field, a man who saw patients every day, and yet he had come all the way to Chandigarh for Karan, and he treated Karan more than a patient. He treated him as a good friend. Karan thought for sure that as his stem cell treatment progressed, he would be shunted off to the side as just another patient. Dr Lox was, of course, a very important man, but he visited often, not only to check up on how Karan's body was healing but to help heal his soul as well. It was as though Dr Lox understood that the pain, which was gradually leaving Karan's hips as the stem cell treatment healed him, had taken residence in his heart instead. It wasn't right for someone so young to be so crippled by life. So, Dr Lox came to cheer him up.

'How's my favourite patient?' Dr Lox greeted him, bustling and cheerful in the silent room. He was brandishing a Tupperware container and grinning widely. Karan couldn't help but grin back.

'I've certainly had better days, Dr Lox, but I'm all the better after seeing you.'

'Glad to see your humour hasn't deserted you. It'd have been a shame.' The doctor consulted with the paperwork that Karan's home health nurse had left, humming to himself as he read. He looked up after a moment, a serious expression on his face.

'Now, listen to me very closely. It's of the utmost importance that you pay very careful attention to me because I'm about to deliver a very serious test that will determine how your treatment is progressing.'

Karan sat up straighter, his eyes on Dr Lox. 'What's wrong?'

Dr Lox kept his face as serious as possible as he explained to Karan what he wanted. 'In this Tupperware container are leftovers of the incredible pilaf my wife made last night. If you eat it and don't think it's the best thing you've ever tasted, then I'm afraid there's nothing I can do for you. You're beyond help.'

Karan laughed, letting out a breath he didn't know he was holding, 'I'm sure it'll do me wonders, Doc. Amit, can you take that to the downstairs kitchen for me? I'll have it for supper if it's not too much trouble.' Amit did as he was told, leaving Karan alone with the doctor.

'Might do you better than anything I can offer,' the doctor joked, pointing at Karan with his pen. 'Stem cell treatment and fancy doctoring is all well and good, but there's nothing like a home-cooked meal and plenty of rest to heal you. Where my healing arts end, the powers of good food and good company can do incredible things.'

Karan nodded, a small smile dancing across his lips. 'If your prescription involves good food, I'll take it. And I can fill it myself. You just wait until I'm out of this bed. I'll cook you a meal like you've never eaten before.'

'I'll hold you to that, Karan,' the doctor said. He finished fiddling with his paperwork and settled at the foot of Karan's bed. 'Now, we need to discuss something serious. And I don't want you to get upset.'

'It's hard for me to get any more upset than I am, Doc. From where I'm sitting, almost any news is good news,' he motioned to the bed, the pills on his nightstand and the monitoring equipment surrounding him.

'Well, this could be a good news depending on how you look at it. But I'm going to need you to seriously consider scheduling a double hip replacement,' The doctor's face was grave as he held Karan's gaze. Karan's heart plummeted into his stomach.

'I thought the stem cell therapy was helping.' *I thought there would be a miracle cure*, he thought to himself. He knew he should have known better than to hold on to hope, but he spent so much time in his fantasy world where he was healthy and strong with Milli, the idea of never being able to walk again without a hip replacement hadn't crossed his mind as a serious possibility.

'The stem cell therapy is helping with the pain but it can only do so much to reverse the damage already caused to your body. There's very little that I can do to heal you beyond this point. If you want to leave this bed—'

'I do. I do more than anything,' Karan responded, trying to keep the note of panic from his voice. He could feel himself slipping into horror.

'The hip replacement is the only way to go, I'm afraid. I can give you a referral to an incredible doctor. We'll get this done the right way,' Dr Lox straightened, clipping the paperwork he had been reviewing to his clipboard.

'Can I have some time alone to think about it?' Karan asked. His thoughts were swimming.

'Of course, Karan. Of course,' the doctor assured him. 'I'll just be downstairs getting my things ready to go. I'll say goodbye before I leave.'

'I'd appreciate that,' Karan said, his voice weak. With that, the doctor left him.

Milli. Of course, she was his first thought in the face of this tragedy. He couldn't leave her hanging again like he had after the car accident. She wouldn't take well to being abandoned like that a second time. If he were to have the hip replacement, and it looked like he would have to have it done, he needed her to know.

But she'll run away, he thought. Like the countless other girls who had seen his scars and found them too frightening to bear. *But what if she doesn't run away?*

Then he might know true love. Then he might not wake up to an empty hospital room. Then something good might happen.

Good things rarely happened to Karan. It was why he tried to keep Milli in the fantasy world they lived in together. He wanted all her sweetness to himself while it would last. His mind wouldn't allow him to process a world in which she would come to him, knowing him for who he was and still loving him. He was afraid that seeing him like this would hurt her terribly.

He could almost hear her voice in his head at that thought. *Shouldn't I have the right to decide how I get hurt?* Especially if that risk of getting hurt was the only thing keeping her from true love. Milli hated to let other people pay for her with little things like dinner dates and plane tickets. To have someone do all the emotional suffering for her without leaving her a choice – she might never forgive him.

He had always asked Milli to be honest with him and now it seemed he could barely be honest himself. He had been lying to her and it needed to stop if they were to have a future together. It seemed so dark in the room suddenly. He wanted to fling open the shades and let in the sunlight. Then, he would call Milli and invite her over.

'Amit!' he called. 'Amit! Please help me!' but there was no response. He sat in bed waiting. 'Dr Lox? Amit? Is anyone there?' Perhaps his voice was too weak. Perhaps his house was too big. Too late he remembered he had sent them both down to the kitchen into the west wing of the house. They couldn't hear him.

He didn't want to wait a moment longer. His hips were feeling better by the day and if they were going to be separated from him soon, he may as well use them while he could. He sat up in bed and slid to the side of the bed on unsteady legs. There was a moment of uncertainty where his hips groaned and he wasn't sure if he was going to make it. But he stood, steadily. It was only four steps to the curtains and four steps back. He could make it. He could do this. Despite the pain shooting through his hips, much worse now that they were supporting him, he could prove to them all that he was independent enough and that he might not need replacements at all.

Step one, step two. By step three he could almost reach the curtains and by step four he had them in his grasp. He tugged them open and let the light flood into his room. Bright and wonderful, the greatest thing he had seen since Milli's face. Illuminating his whole world, his situation. Let it. Let everyone see. Milli had the right to know. He turned back to the bed, where his phone was, and took another step.

Step five. And he crashed to the floor. There was no step six.

EIGHT

Water spurted from the kitchen faucet filling the large mason jar. The sight of it, crystal clear and shimmering in the sunlight, made Milli smile. With the weather close to boiling and the sun shining down on the lawn, she had settled on a plan for the day: brew a little sun tea, pull a lawn chair out into the shade, and re-read her favourite novel on her day off. The well-worn paperback was waiting for her on the kitchen table. All she had to do was pop a couple of tea bags into the jar, screw the lid on tight, and leave it to soak up the sun while she lost herself in the pages of her favourite fantasy.

Well, her second favourite fantasy. Her new favourite fantasy, a life with Karan, was coming so close to becoming a reality she could taste it. It was hard to paint a clear picture in her mind of the life he led when he was being so mysterious, but everything she knew about him, she loved. She couldn't help herself. He was a brilliant man: cultured, fine, and sophisticated. He pursued knowledge like she knew boys to pursue girls in short shorts. He was well read and well dressed. Whenever she had a question, he seemed to know something about it. Whenever he puzzled over something, Milli always had thoughts to offer in return. He stimulated her mind. He made her laugh. They were intellectual equals. Milli had resigned herself to being misunderstood all her life but she had found someone who kindled a fire in her. She wouldn't let him go. She wouldn't let anyone tear her away from him.

She worried about the secret that she could sense he was keeping from her, the one last thing keeping them apart. She knew it wasn't something horrible, like a wife on the side or connections to crime. She knew Karan. There was an innocence to him, a sweetness in the way he spoke to her, that let her know that he was a good man. But still, there was something separating them. She knew because every time she mentioned meeting him, he seemed to balk. He hid his face from her, skittish as a horse when she mentioned wanting to see it.

It wasn't that she was coming on too strong or that he didn't like her. He seemed to want nothing more than to be with her. When they spoke, he fantasized about her resting her head on his chest as the two of them gazed up at the stars. He fantasized about holding her hand and running his fingers through her hair. She could nearly feel his touch when he spoke to her. So why was he holding back? What made him hold back?

It was clear that he was suffering and that he didn't want her to know. His voice sounded weak on the phone sometimes. He was tired from long days at work, he told her, but she knew it was more than that. His soul was as lonely as hers. It wore a person down and whatever suffering he had, she wanted to help him through it. But she couldn't make him understand just how badly she wanted to be there for him. Her heart longed for him. She would fight monsters for him, knowing he would do the same for her. But this wasn't one of Milli's paperbacks. The monsters of the real world were far more dangerous than those in print.

Whatever it was, Milli would wait for him to reveal it to her. She had been honest with him and knew that he would be honest with her in good time. It was what they had built their relationship on and it would serve them until the end. In the end, Milli hoped that she would be holding Karan's hand, and not just smiling as he spoke to her on the phone.

When Milli woke up that morning to an empty house, she had been overjoyed at first, too excited by the thought of a morning alone to wonder where her mother had gone. Having a day off, finally free from her mother's stony gaze and ice-cold comments that she threw like knives at Milli, seemed almost too good to be true. Her mother was beyond disappointed with her for how things went with Rahull and wasn't speaking to Milli, unless it was to insult her.

But Milli couldn't bring herself to care. Rahull was a pig, an uninspiring lout of a boy. Even if she had wanted to love him, she couldn't bring her heart to feel something it didn't feel. It was a shame that her mother didn't understand. But it was hard for her mother to understand anything beyond acquiring more pills and passing out in a stoned stupor.

Carrying the jar of tea in one arm and her paperback in the other, Milli made her way to the porch. She was determined not to let her mother's bitter mood sour her day. She would instead stretch out in the light and enjoy her favourite story. Anything to help her forget the haunted house behind her where her mother roamed listlessly, knocking things over in the middle of the night, a corpse still inhabited by the ghost of a woman who had once been so caring and loving towards Milli.

It felt like an exorcism to have her mother absent from the house. The air was lighter around her. Easier to breathe. It seemed to Milli as though her mother was staying at home more often than not lately during the times when Milli was also at home. Clearly something about having switched from third shift to first shift made it so that their paths crossed more often. Seeing her mother more often allowed Milli to see just how bad her condition had gotten but also left her feeling more trapped in their dilapidated house than ever before. And it was a claustrophobic life. It felt like it was the only one she had ever known.

The life that she dreamed of for herself and Karan was nothing like this. It had wide open spaces. Nothing could tie them down. They only needed each other. There was nothing holding them back. No sick mothers, no strange secrets, no Rahull. They would live in the same time zone. They would conquer the same fears. They would do it all, his hand in hers.

If only he could muster the courage to take her hand in his.

Then her phone buzzed on the arm of her lawn chair, a reminder to Milli that she could never truly be free from a world in which she was so heavily submerged. There was something about the way her phone buzzed when Rahull was on the other end that let her know that it was him calling instead of someone she actually wanted to speak with. It was as though the machine itself was irritated by his presence in its contacts. But perhaps Milli was just projecting.

She turned the ringer to silent until his call disconnected. She didn't have the excuse of being at work and she didn't care. She was sure if he wanted to, he could see her sunning herself on the lawn from his back porch. It was so hard to ward him off when he lived so close and had been trying to move closer still, all his life. It was why either Milli or he would have to leave. But he was stubborn and Milli was trapped in her mother's dark world—it seemed as if they were at an impasse. He was circling closer with every passing moment, vulture-like.

Lately, Milli wondered if he could replace her with someone else who might love him in a way Milli was never able to. It was so frustrating to her, to have someone in her life who thought he loved her, when really he just wanted to feel her love him. A man who loved her would act like Karan did—would teach her things, would listen to her talk about her feelings and the things in her life that scared her. A man who truly loved her would wait patiently for her to reveal herself to him instead of demanding that she put her full life on view for him, tragedies and sufferings and all, like some kind of a sick striptease.

A moment later, her text notification pinged. She rolled her eyes. As usual, he was going to just bombard her with texts about whatever was on his mind, then berate her for ignoring him if she didn't immediately respond. Because, of course, she was such a good listener, and that meant she had to listen to whatever insane thought he had to offer. She wondered what it was this time.

She got her answer just a moment later.

Just wanted to apologize, call me back.

Milli, I'm sorry for how I acted. Please forgive me.

I think I'm just desperate and it's—

The last message looked as though it had been sent prematurely. Milli couldn't help but marvel at it. Rahull admitting something about himself that didn't have anything to do with his stunning masculinity, mediocre prospects, and how clearly he was meant for Milli because of some strange fluke of fate that had allowed them to grow up together in the same small town. What were the chances? Perhaps the world was ending on this gorgeous summer day.

She couldn't disagree with him though. He was desperate. They all were, growing up here in this one horse town. Looking for a way out, a way up, a way to something better. It wasn't Milli's fault that the only thing he had seen when he looked around was her. She had done nothing but try hard all her life to escape her own hell. She didn't have time to pull Rahull out of his misery when she was so close to the fresh air of day.

And that was what he didn't understand, what she couldn't make him understand no matter how she tried. She wasn't going to be his saviour and no matter how many fantasies he had, he was never going to be hers. They had to save themselves. Getting married and trying to force a relationship because of some vague notion he had harboured since they were children was a sure-fire way to trap them both in these rundown houses until they had rotted more thoroughly than the walls.

Silence from her phone, finally, as Milli came back around to the one strong feeling she always had for Rahull: pure pity underlying all the irritation and disgust she felt towards him. Because she knew he was capable of doing better, of rising above this situation and becoming a good man. He was a hard worker; he was devoted to his family. He would devote himself solely to her if she would let him. But he would do this only in exchange for her adoration, her submission to the avalanche of tangled feelings he had for her. And she couldn't – wouldn't – do that to either of them. She only wished that he would learn to love himself as strongly as he thought he loved her.

It was then that Milli's phone buzzed. An incoming call that she knew wasn't Rahull's for he was too embarrassed to try and phone again so soon. She looked at it, a wide smile blossoming reflexively across her face. She thought for a sweet moment that it was Karan calling her, ready to listen to her talk about her day, her novel, and the other things in her life. Instead, an unfamiliar number with a Chandigarh area code flashed across the screen. Milli answered the phone with a deep sense of foreboding, afraid that she might hear the worst. After her brother died, it was all unfamiliar phone numbers and condolence calls. She couldn't handle that again. If it was the police, telling her that her mother was lost forever, Milli wasn't certain what she would do. Break down, maybe, and pray that Karan would be there to help her.

Instead, a polite voice across the phone line asked Milli for her mother.

'She isn't here but I'm her daughter,' Milli said. 'Can I take the message?'

'This is the number that we were given to call on, for the mortgage of the account number ending in 5559,' the teller told Milli. 'She is behind on payment and we want to know why.'

Milli felt her heart sink. 'There must be some mistake,' she replied. 'Our house is over one hundred and fifty years old. It's been in the family before since I was born. There is no way that we have taken out a mortgage on this home.'

'Unfortunately, ma'am, it seems to be the case. Your home has been mortgaged for over a year now. This is the Bajwa residence, is it not?' The voice on the other end was professional, impersonal. As though he wasn't delivering the worst news of Milli's life so far. First her brother, then her mother, and now the very home in which she lived.

The millstone in Milli's stomach grew heavier by the moment. 'It is,' she replied. 'How far behind are we on the mortgage?'

'I'm afraid that I'm not at liberty to give that information over the phone,' the teller said. 'But I can tell you that your home is in grave danger of repossession should you fall further behind.'

'Where did you say that your bank was located? I will be right down to sort out this mess. Don't worry, everything will be okay,' she said this mostly to herself and not to the teller on the other end. She had some extra money put away in case of an emergency, although she hadn't anticipated this one. She could make this work. Things might be tight for a while but she could make them work.

Milli hung up the phone with a sigh, feeling a tightness in her chest that was threatening to spike into panic. Abandoning the sun tea on the porch, Milli ran through the house like a woman possessed. First, she opened her purse to check how much cash she had squirrelled away there, trying to get a full understanding of her finances. Shock ran through her body as she realized that her wallet was empty and her cards were splayed across her purse, as though some common thug had ransacked her wallet in a rush. But her purse had been in the house all day and the night before that. She remembered hearing her mother storming through the house late last night, sounding as though she were turning the house up on its end. Suddenly, it all began to make sense. Her mother had been stealing.

Milli's heart sank before she had even gotten to the jar underneath her bed. It had been her secret hiding spot for money since she was a child, a slit sliced into its plastic lid where she could deposit cash for a rainy day. She had kept upwards of a fifty thousand rupees tucked there just in case. She wasn't sure what she was hoping to find in the jar today. A miracle, maybe. But the jar was empty, filled with nothing but aire. Nothing but fragments of the broken lid.

'Oh, no,' Milli said to herself. 'Oh no. This can't be.'

But it was. Suddenly the answers to the many questions Milli had became clear as day. Her mother was home at odd hours and rarely gone longer than an hour at a time. That was not nearly long enough to take a shift at the hospital. The large amount of pills that she still managed to swallow every day made perfect sense as she had nowhere else to be and nothing else to do. Milli's suspicions that her mother had been fired were answered with a simple call to the hospital.

'Oh, honey … ' her mother's old shift leader began when Milli asked the woman where her mother was. 'We sent her home weeks ago. Months, even.' She let the phone fall back on the table with a clatter, the nurse's voice tiny on the other line. 'Hello? Milli? Hello?'

Her mother's addiction had already cost them everything and now it was about to lose them their home. But Milli couldn't let that happen. Even if her mother had stolen everything that she had, Milli would still find a way to keep the place she loved. Even when she hated it, home was home. And even though the ghost of her mother who haunted the home had turned against her, Milli would still protect what was hers to protect. She would not lose this home.

But first she had to find her mother.

She looked in the fields beyond their home first. Sometimes on a day like today, her mother would lay out in the open air and enjoy the breeze. Perhaps she had passed out and had not yet awakened. Milli stood on the porch with her hands on her hips. She scanned the fields around her with a keen eye but saw nothing out of the ordinary. Her mother was not there. She had no idea where her mother could be.

Unsure of what else to do, Milli picked up her phone. When she called her mother's phone it went straight to voicemail. She had suspected that it would. Her mother was hard to reach these days, even with new technology. She was often too high to remember to charge the thing, so it sat like a brick on the coffee table. Milli let out a groan of frustration, feeling urgency pulsing through her body. If her mother was not at home, where was she? Had Milli really been so consumed with Karan's life that she had forgotten about her mother? No, Milli was not to blame for her mother's illness. She knew that. Even when she had to remind herself.

She fumbled with the phone for a moment, not sure what her next step should be. Should she call the police? Should she call the bank once more? There were too many unknown factors here. Her mother had disappeared. That much was evident. But what else did she really know about it? Her money was gone. Her house was mortgaged. Her mother's drug problem was clearly worse than she could even begin to imagine. What could she do? Who could she call?

Finally, Milli did the only thing that her heart had been able to tell her to do. She lifted the phone to her ear, listening to the ring of the phone on the other line. She waited for someone to answer it, knowing that he would. He had promised he would never abandon her again. Karan would know what to do. He always did.

Milli was aware of for the first time, that Karan was not the only one keeping a secret. She had barely revealed the first thing about her mother's crippling addiction to him. She had kept her mother's secret and now it was coming back to crucify her. She could only hope that when she was honest with Karan, he would be just as honest with her in return.

The phone rang, and rang, and rang. Milli listened, the sense of dread in her stomach threatening to completely overwhelm her. Why wasn't Karan answering his phone?

NINE

The anxiety that throbbed in Milli's chest from the moment she took the bank's phone call had become a raging beast trying to break its way out of her rib cage. She had hoped only for Karan's calming voice at the other end of the line, praying that he would comfort her and calm her down until she could explain to him what had happened. She had imagined that he would help her breathe again, his sweet voice in her ear helping her to think through the problem and find a solution. But he hadn't answered the phone.

Milli had no time for heartbreak. She couldn't worry about Karan. Maybe he had some other appointment or an emergency. Usually, he answered her phone call within the first couple of rings no matter what time of the day it was, but he was a busy man and usually it was he who called her whenever he had a free moment. So, it would be okay, she kept reminding herself. He would call her back soon enough. She would just have to get through the minutes until he came back to her.

Her mother was missing. Her mother had stolen a considerable sum of money from her. Her mother had mortgaged their home, gambled away the place where they had made every memory they had together and risked ruining their lives forever. All for a bottle of pills? A gram of heroin? Just how bad had her mother's addiction gotten while Milli was busy trying to make ends meet and devoting the rest of her time to Karan?

At a different point in her life, Milli might have felt guilty but now she understood that her mother's choices were hers alone. Still, she couldn't help but try to negotiate her way out of the tragedy her mother was forcing her to live. If only her brother had survived his tour as a soldier. If only he had been around to help her mother and repair their crumbling house ...

Milli sank into the rocking chair on the porch, watching the sun tea growing darker and the shadows growing longer in the yard. She did not know how long she sat there, rocking furiously as she tried to find solution to their problems in vain. A second job couldn't save them now, even without the failing mortgage. The repairs to the house alone were far beyond what they had been able to afford. And God forbid if Milli couldn't find her mother alive, the cost of a funeral...

She shook her head. This wasn't a nightmare yet; it was just an unpleasant afternoon. Some miracle would happen. Something would save them. She just couldn't figure out what that thing could be yet.

Karan still hadn't returned her call, although that was one of the furthest things from her mind. But no one else had called her back yet either. She reckoned no news was good news. She would put out a couple of calls to the local barflies, the supermarket, the gambling hall, the hospital where her mother used to work and even a couple of churches and temples in the area in case her mother had finally found religion. No one seemed to know where her mother could possibly be. Milli wasn't ready to start combing the fields, the woods and the railroad tracks just yet. She would give her mother a bit of time to rouse herself and come home. After all, weren't you supposed to wait twenty-four hours before you filed a missing person report? Milli wasn't sure. But she wasn't sure of anything just now.

She could feel tears welling in her eyes. Everything was in shambles around her and it took all she had to not break down. Imagining Karan's arms around her and his voice in her ear, his gentle smile and his strong hands couldn't calm her. She needed him here in person. She needed to be held. But she knew no one was coming to save her.

So Milli straightened in the rocking chair. Bringing herself to her feet, she let her eyes close for a moment. She centred herself, breathing out through her nose until she felt strength flowing back into her body. She could handle this. She had handled things like this before. It was a challenge, not a problem. Her mother would be fine. She would find a way to fix the mortgage situation. All the impossible things weighing her down, she could solve.

Then she heard a cough from the other side of the porch and all that strength failed her once more.

She turned her head and there was Rahull, awkward and massive, standing on the porch. He seemed more nervous than she had ever seen him, even more nervous than the night he had come to her house after her brother died. He had been skittish then, jumping at the slightest sound in the old house like an intruder hoping his presence wouldn't be noticed. He had handled her too gently, as though she were something breakable instead of highly broken, until she had screamed at him to leave her alone. His shirt was tucked into his waistband and his face was clean. It looked as though he had even run a comb through his hair.

Whatever fresh hell he was about to put Milli through, she didn't have time for it today.

'Do you know where my mother is?' she snapped at him. She could barely keep the accent she had spent so many years hiding out of her voice. She was angry and scared, and he could hear it in the way she spoke. He raised his hands in subservience.

'I haven't seen her since the last time we ran into each other at the market. Why?'

Milli guffawed, kicking at a loose board on the porch. 'I don't believe this. I don't believe you at all. The way you're so buddy-buddy with her all the time—' gears started turning in Milli's head, spitting out possibilities faster than she could voice them. Her mind was a whirl of misery and fear.

'You've been helping her score, haven't you?' she hissed at him, looking for signs of guilt in his face.

He snorted a laugh, 'Milli, don't kid around.'

'Oh, I assure you, I'm not joking.'

He looked around the place, eyeing the crooked fence and the sloping roof with distaste. 'Something's really got your goat and for once I don't think it's me,' he ran a finger along the peeling paint of the porch. For some reason that was the final straw for Milli: how dare he show up in her hour of need only to judge, dismiss and belittle her? She couldn't hate him more if she tried. Milli seethed, all her worry and frustration turned to rage. She wanted to knock Rahull off the porch and send him rolling down the hill back to his place, never to return again. Perhaps that would wipe the smug expression off his face.

'Rahull Suri, if you don't know where my mother is, I'd appreciate it if you'd get in your car, get off my property and not come back until you've found her,' Milli said, deceptively sweet enough to smother the anger she felt inside her. If she could get him out of here, maybe she could actually focus on the situation at hand. But he didn't seem swayed by the saccharine in her voice. Instead, he took a step towards her, his face uncharacteristically serious. It unnerved Milli more than her missing mother or any of the day's other various troubles.

'Milli, I promise that just as soon as you answer this question for me, I'll be out of your hair. I'll even find your mother for you, although why you insist on dragging her back from the edge every time she wants to throw herself off, I'll never understand.'

'Don't ever talk about my mother that way, Rahull. It isn't your place.'

He held his hands up once more, 'I know, I know. I just need to hear one thing from you: Milli Bajwa, do you really want to live on this hill for the rest of your life, rescuing your mother whenever she needs rescuing and getting older by the minute?'

'How's that question going to help me find my mother?' she crossed her arms over her chest, angling her hip. It was a stance that had frightened Rahull off many a time when they were just children on the playground together. But now he didn't budge.

'Answer the question, please,' he said, his voice strangely quiet. Milli could only think that she did not like where this was going.

'No, I don't. You're not as stupid as you look, Rahull, so why are you asking me a foolish question like that?' she rolled her eyes and turned away. 'You know what, don't even bother going to look for her. I can find her myself. I swear, sometimes you're—'

She stopped mid-sentence when she turned back to Rahull and saw him down on one knee. It must have been difficult for him to lower his massive body into that position. In his great paw of a hand he held a delicate black velvet box with its lid propped open. Inside the box was a plain gold band with a tiny diamond on it. Milli's heart sank at the sight of it.

'Milli Bajwa, I've been hoping to take you away from this place even since we were children. I've been working hard and saving all my life to make a name for myself, and even though I've done that and more, you still won't give me the time of a day. But I can make you love me. Give it some time and you'll come to see the kind of man I really am. Please, marry me.'

For the first time, looking into his eyes, she did see the kind of man he was. Perhaps she had known all along. He was a smart and hardworking man. The kind of man who could make a girl happy for the rest of her life. But he was not the man for her.

'I'll never love you, Rahull,' she said it as kindly as possible, but she needed him to understand that it was the truth. 'Not ever. No matter where I am, where you take me, or what you do for me. I am not the woman for you. You'll find her one day, i know you will, but you need to understand that she is not me.' She wanted him to get off his knees, to tell her he understood and to leave her alone. Maybe, in time, there wouldn't be any hard feelings between them. But she knew that of all the things she had felt about Rahull over the years, love had never been one of them. And it never would be.

A thundercloud fell across Rahull's face as he slowly got to his feet. It occurred to Milli, not for the first time, just how big Rahull was. When his shoulders tensed and his face darkened, she was afraid. He could quite easily hurl her off the porch.

Instead, he punched the siding of their house, hard. Paint flecks embedded in his knuckles and littered the floor of the porch. 'Rahull, don't, it's in bad enough shape already,' she said worriedly, backing away. She wasn't sure what to do. He advanced towards her and for one awful moment, Milli felt true fear.

But then, Rahull collected himself. He had the good sense to look ashamed. 'I'm sorry,' he said, motioning to the porch. 'I … I'm sorry.'

'It's okay,' she said quickly, hoping that her voice wouldn't shake as she spoke, 'but I'd like you to leave now, please.'

'Okay,' he said. 'Okay,' he repeated, taking two steps towards his car, still idling in her driveway, before stopping to glance back at her.

'I'm not taking no for an answer just yet, Milli. I think you're making a mistake. I'll give you time to think it over. I'll let you decide if this is really the kind of life you want.' With that he was gone, his car rumbling back down the gravel driveway before disappearing down the road as though he had never been there at all.

Milli's shoulders sagged in relief, her breath coming just a little easier now that he was gone. His final words to her made her afraid, but she had to cast that fear aside for now. She did the only thing she knew how to do to destroy her fear. She composed a text to Karan.

I'm so afraid, the text read. *I wish I could see you. Please. Just let me hold you.*

She did not expect him to respond and was shocked when her phone buzzed only a moment after she sent the text. Even more surprising to Milli was Karan's response.

It wasn't any words. It was an address.

Milli didn't need to be told twice. Hopping into her sedan, she plugged the address into her phone's GPS and tore down the road. *Karan,* she thought. *Karan. I'm coming.*

TEN

The sun was low in the sky when Milli left her home, hopping into the car without a second thought. Her mind was on Karan and Karan alone. She needed him now more than ever and he had invited her over just in her time of need. The clouds were tinged with orange and pink. It was a beautiful evening in Chandigarh, all cantaloupe-coloured light and the earliest spray of stars winking in the sky. The shadows grew longer, coating the world around her in hazy twilight by the time she pulled up in front of a mansion larger than anything she had ever seen.

Her GPS told her she was at the right place but even her GPS sometimes made mistakes. She had understood that Karan was rich. His outlook on life, his taste in food, his spontaneous airline adventure that had landed him in Paris had all clued her in early to the fact that they were definitely from different economic classes. However, it hadn't bothered her because his mind and his passion drew her in far more than his finances ever could. But now, gazing at what must be his home, she was a little blindsided.

Rich to her meant expensive wine and shiny watches. The home she was looking at wasn't just two storeys worth of new money and an outdoor pool. It was a palace, an estate with rolling fields that looked to Milli like heaven on earth. This wasn't just a nice salary and a fitted suit. This was wealth and power, true and intoxicating. It frightened Milli a little. She looked down at her pilled sun dress and checked her messy hair in the rear-view mirror. She was no pampered beauty queen. Would she even fit in this beautiful home?

But Karan had seen something in her that had caught his eye like no glittering diamond or precious metal ever had. He had made it clear to Milli with everything he had said and done for her that he found her far more beautiful than the swans in his pond or the glittering gate marking the entrance to his estate. He had treated her with nothing but respect all the days they had known each other.

It was obvious to Milli now, gazing at his incredible estate, just how much he truly valued her. She was more valuable to Karan than all the jewels and wealth of the world. His appraisal of her worth was just Karan being honest. By now, Milli had got a brief idea that Karan had known nothing but wealth for all of his life. A man of hard work and great reward, of first class plane tickets and expensive cologne, found Milli to be indispensable. That he had grown up among all this opulence and found her the most valuable thing in all of his life warmed her heart.

She hesitated for only a moment before pressing the call button on the gate. There was a long, pleasant buzz before a fuzzy voice on the other end of the line answered.

'Singhania residence,' the man at the other end stated. Although the voice was masked by the static in the connection she could tell it was not Karan.

'Yes, hi,' Milli said, putting on her best customer-service voice. 'I was sent this address by a man named Karan. I wondered whether I'm at the right location.'

There was no response from the other end except another electric buzz from the call box. The gates swung open and Milli didn't want to waste any time in confusion or fear. She wanted to be with Karan. She put her car back into gear, embarrassed by her old, shoddy sedan as she pulled into the driveway. It was a long, winding road leading past what appeared to be a guest house and onwards to the main house. Milli glimpsed at a large, shuttered garage that no doubt held countless luxury cars. She felt out of place and underdressed amidst this extravagance. But still. she was here for Karan and nothing else. And she had been allowed past the gates, so she must be where he is.

The sense of dread and excitement, anticipation and nerves, all mingled in her body. She tried to quell it by focusing instead on the love she felt for Karan growing warm and confident in her bones.

The main house was mostly semi dark. Only a couple of lights were glowing upstairs and that must be where Karan was, she assumed. The feeling that she was so close to meeting him, so close to realizing her dreams and fantasies, swamped her with emotions and tears welled in her eyes. She was so close to him but she hadn't yet seen his face.

She knocked at the door once, then thought better of it and rang the bell at the side of the doorway. She felt hesitant, uncertain and afraid. The courage that she had felt upon receiving his message, that had inspired her to climb into her car and drive off into the unknown without a second thought, was failing her. But it was too late to walk away. She had to face her fears. Karan was on the other side of that door, her reward for surviving all that had happened today. She would be in his arms soon enough. She took a deep breath.

The door opened.

To her surprise the man who answered the door was a well-dressed, elderly gentleman with neatly-trimmed white hair. He seemed tired. However, the smile he offered Milli was as warm as sunshine. He caught her off guard. This couldn't be Karan, could it?

'If you'll follow me, Milli, I'll take you to Karan,' the man said. Milli nodded wordlessly, fidgeting as she went. She couldn't remember telling the man her name, but she supposed Karan must have told him – his father? His … butler? Milli had never had staff leading her through a house like this before. But then again, she had never been in a house so big that she was afraid of getting lost.

Milli smoothed down her dress and ran her fingers through her hair, unsure of what else she could do to spruce herself up. She felt very out of place, but she tried to reassure herself by telling herself that at the end of this journey was the place where she belonged: in Karan's arms. She stayed close to the man as he moved quickly through a labyrinth of corridors. She had already lost her bearings and wondered where Karan was.

She passed by a portrait of a family hanging in the hall. A regal woman and her husband with two small children, a chubby-cheeked baby girl, doe-eyed and laughing, and a more serious-looking young boy with dark eyes and curly hair, with a mischievous edge to his smile. It echoed a happier time, a house filled with warmth and laughter. The house in the painting was nothing like the house she was in now, save for the trim in the background was the same trim of the great hall from where she had entered. It had been painted in this same mansion.

It struck her that in spite of the opulence of the house on the outside, on the inside it was in fact one of the coldest places she had ever been. Goosebumps rose on her arms as she followed the man up a flight of stairs. The halls appeared sterile and impersonal, nothing to suggest that this home had had a woman's caring touch in the recent times. She could imagine it in a different time. A little colour on the walls, some brighter lighting, some open windows. Maybe a vase of flowers on an end table here and there.

But there was no time to fantasize about crafting a warm and lovely home for Karan to live in. The man opened the door to a room and invited Milli in with a gesture.

She almost couldn't comprehend the sight before her eyes. The bedroom was something in between a master suite and a hospital room. A beautiful full-length mirror on the ceiling reflected up the sight of a man lying unconscious in the bed. The bedside table had a little pile of books on it, some bottles of pills and a vase of wilting flowers.

The strange beeping sound she heard over the phone, it took her a moment to register, was from the monitors hooked up to the bed. In the bed was the most beautiful man she had ever beheld. He was model handsome with the strong, chiselled jaw she had been dreaming of for months. Even with his mouth slack in sleep and his body small beneath the huge amount of medical equipment supporting him, he was angelic in rest. She was so caught up in the rise and fall of his chest that it took her a second to see the bandage wrapped around his head. Finally, it all came together in her head.

'Karan,' she breathed, her eyes swimming with tears.

'I bet you were wondering why he called you here today of all days,' the old man said softly. Milli flinched. She had forgotten he was there at all.

'Please, sit down,' he motioned to a chair by the bed. Milli settled into it gratefully. Now that she was closer to the sleeping man, she noticed a hypertrophic scar on his chest. Not one that could have been made by accident but a precise surgical scar.

'What happened to him?' she asked. It hurt her to see him in this state. Her hands fluttered with anxiety, wanting to go to him, to touch his skin, but afraid she might hurt him worse.

'It's a long story,' the man replied. He pulled up a chair across from her and began to speak.

ELEVEN

Milli listened numbly as the man, Amit, began his explanation of Karan's tumultuous life. Through the course of his narrative, there were moments where he faltered, eyes glistening with tears and his voice fraught with emotion as he relayed the struggles Karan had undergone. Milli could understand why. Amit had been in Karan's life ever since it began: employed by Karan's father and later by Karan himself. He was an honorary member of the family and it warmed Milli to hear how Karan's folks loved him. In stark contrast, her own family couldn't stay together even though they hadn't faced half the hardship Karan had faced since he was a six-month-old babe in arms. She was glad to know that his parents had remained impregnable to his suffering.

'The diagnosis was hyperlipidaemia, a rare cholesterol disease. Even more rare was how it affected him from infancy. Most of us don't have to worry about our cholesterol until we're a whole lot older' Amit chuckled softly, referencing his own age, before his face grew serious again.

'By the time Karan began to crawl, he had undergone more tests than most people undergo in their lifetime. To see him, so tiny on the table like that, reaching for his mother as they drew blood samples from his tiny veins … a man never forgets it,' he said sadly.

'But Karan was resilient from the day he was born,' Amit resumed, finding strength in his voice even as he said it. 'He healed and grew into a wonderful little boy. The light and joy of his parents' world. I remember his little sister and him running around this stuffy old mansion, laughing and playing. They brightened up these halls. This home was a different place back then. Not so gloomy or cold. Karan and his sister were like sunbeams.'

Milli could envision the bright, boisterous, curly-haired, laughing boy that Karan once was, running through the halls of this mansion. It warmed her heart to think of him that way. She always had a soft spot for children. As a child, she had always been rather quiet and had tried to make herself as inconspicuous as possible. The idea of a child blossoming in this environment made her smile. It seemed like a great place to grow up.

'However, before he was ten years old, disaster struck again,' Amit continued, his face growing grey with the pain of the memory. 'His heart began to buckle under the weight of all the cholesterol that his body produced. He grew sick and weak. The doctors told him that a heart murmur in his aortic valve was causing leakage. An aortic valve stenosis was needed to save his life. I wish I'd never heard the words.

'They explained that if he did not get the valve replacement promptly it could prove fatal for the young lad. They postponed the surgery with medication for as long as possible so that they could insert an adult valve in due course; for a few years, it seemed to work. But unfortunately, there was nothing more that they could do for him. He was in the operating theatre for open heart surgery – a procedure that most men don't have to undergo until their seventies – before he was eighteen.'

When Milli was eighteen, she had been free to do as she liked. Stealing her brother's car keys at midnight and driving through the dark just to find a spot under the stars to sit had been her favourite thing to do. Her biggest worry was her mother's volatility and her brother's impending tour with the army. They had seemed like enormous worries at the time but it was nothing in comparison to undergoing an open heart surgery.

'We thought he would have a reprieve for a while, that the surgery had worked and the strong, healthy young man he'd grown into would be able to enjoy the rewards of life. He had certainly earned it by going through the hell of his childhood. But the damned doctors …' Amit swore before realizing he was in the presence of a lady and had the grace to look abashed. But Milli didn't care. She would have cursed, too. The thought of the suffering the man in the bed had been through before he was a man made her sick to her stomach.

'When they'd opened him up they must have seen the two blockages in his heart instead of one, but they did nothing about it,' the fury in his voice was evident. Milli bit her tongue as she forced herself to listen quietly. It was hard to focus on anything but the beautiful man resting on the bed, face fretful in sleep. She wanted to smooth away the worry on his face that his bad dreams caused. She wanted to crawl into his arms, to pepper kisses across his face until he woke up and she could see the beautiful colour of his eyes. She wanted to run a finger over the scar across his chest, the physical evidence of how brave he had had to be for so long.

'They had to perform open heart surgery again on him when he was nineteen. The doctors said he had a ten per cent chance of survival. I remember before he went under, he joked that he'd come back to haunt them if he died and not in a Casper sort of way,' Amit chuckled at the memory.

'Within ten months, he'd gone under the knife twice with one of the most invasive procedures a person can undergo,' Amit continued, his voice hoarse with pain. 'I thought it would kill his mother, to watch him undergo so many trials and tribulations.

I thought it would break his father. I held his sister as she cried in the waiting room and thought there was no way this family could make it through this. But Karan's strength carried all of us. Through all of this, he never lost his sense of humour. He never gave up. And above all, he still hoped for the future.'

A smile flitted across Amit's face as he spoke. 'Despite his health troubles, Karan grew into an incredible young man. He shouldered his father's legacy with an immense sense of pride and accomplishment and helped develop his business into the flourishing corporation it is today. He always had a joke to tell and a smile on his lips. His sunny disposition was infectious. Of course, he developed a taste for the finer things in life. Fast cars, incredible cuisine, expensive cologne, pretty women ...'

Milli laughed. This sounded like the Karan she knew. Now everything made sense. The suffering and loneliness. The pain had only made him kinder. If she thought she loved him before, she knew for sure that she did now. It was all she could do not to take him in her arms right there and then.

'You have to understand where Karan's coming from, with women. Why he kept his suffering from you for so long. These awful women who came and went so quickly I could barely keep track of them, when all Karan wanted was someone to stay. With his fortune and his loneliness, he attracted a lot of ... ' Amit steepled his hands, considering how best to phrase it, '... gold-diggers. Women who saw him as a pay check. As a means to an end, when all he ever saw in them was a person who might love him.' Amit sighed.

It made even more sense to Milli why he had hidden so much from her in the beginning. Although he was strong, there was a lot of him that was vulnerable. And it was apparent that those vulnerable places had been hurt by women with hearts colder than ice. The fact that these women had taken such blatant advantage of his gentle nature, his suffering and his aspiration for love, disgusted her. How cold could one be? Perhaps Milli was biased but it seemed to her that falling in love with Karan was barely a choice at all for her. All she had had to do was speak to him once and she had been irresistibly drawn to him. How wicked were these women that they could feel nothing for him, and that they could use him like that?

'It was why I decided to text you from Karan's phone, Milli,' Amit said. That got her attention. 'When he had his latest accident, a head injury from falling, he was getting ready to dial your number. He was going to take the courageous step to see you. I had to fulfil what he'd started. I've been with Karan all his life. I understand how his mind works. And I think what he has with you is the strongest chance he's had of happiness in his life. I think you could be his true love.'

Milli's head swam to know why he had been trying to contact her before his latest injury. He had sworn he would never leave her, and it was true: he never would. The words 'true love' echoed in her head. She had always known that Karan was special but thinking of him as 'the one', as her true love … it felt good. It felt right. She believed it. She now had utmost good faith that the man lying there in that bed was really the man for her, come hell or high water.

'And I think he could be my true love,' she said softly. He nodded as though she had confirmed something that he had suspected all along.

'Well, then, Milli, there's something you need to know,' he said, his face serious. 'I needed to know that you loved him before I revealed this to you. His suffering in this bed isn't just from the head injury or from the problems with his heart. The hyperlipidaemia has taken more from him than just his heart. It's also taken his ability to walk.'

'I…I don't understand…' Milli was stunned. The man in the bed couldn't have been older than thirty, and indeed looked much younger. How could he be robbed of his ability to walk in the prime of his life?

'There was a car accident. A bad one. Just a few days ago, when he was coming home from Paris.'

Suddenly Milli remembered the week-long silence when Karan hadn't contacted her. She thought he had left her but the reality was so much worse. She couldn't imagine the suffering he had endured all alone. She wished desperately to have been by his side, to have been there to hold his hand and protect him while he healed. But Amit wasn't finished explaining yet.

'During his MRI, the doctors saw something strange in his hips. It seemed that Karan had been hiding the pain he was in for quite some time. He did not take the pain he had been going through seriously until he was told by the doctors that he was suffering from avascular necrosis. Essentially, bone death in his hips as a result of the cholesterol building in his body.' Milli flinched as she came to understand just what Karan was dealing with. The poor man seemed to have the worst luck of anyone she had ever met. What a horrible thing for a young man to have to suffer.

'Not only was the pain so bad that it left him nearly bedridden, but it was irreversible. With stem cell therapy recommended by Dr Lox, who has been a lifesaver thus far with his good humour and wise advice throughout this hell, he has been able to reduce the pain. But I'm afraid his suffering isn't over just yet,' Amit said. 'He will need a double hip replacement if he is ever to dream of walking again, and even then, it won't be without assistance for a long time. He'll need intensive physiotherapy. It will take a while before he can think of walking unaided.'

'Wow,' Milli said. It was all she could say. Her heart felt full the first time she saw Karan's face, and now she could feel it breaking for him. His suffering was so immense. That he was able to love at all was a miracle. She only wished she could absorb some of his pain.

'If this frightens you, if you don't think you can handle it, I'd rather you left before he woke up and didn't contact him again. It's easier that way. I don't think he can survive another heartbreak, Milli,' Amit said sombrely, staring deep into her eyes. She understood how serious he was. It would be so easy to walk away now. She was being offered a way out. She could take it.

But if she did, could her heart survive being apart from Karan? She didn't think so. If she left him, she would never feel such love again. Yes, his love came at a high price. She would have to watch him suffer from pains she couldn't heal. Until death did them part.

But wasn't it worth it? To kiss him. To hold him. To be with him. Milli knew it was. She didn't hesitate with her response to Amit.

'No. I love him. I don't want to be apart from him. This seems hard. But I'll go through hell if it means we can go through life together,' she replied. Amit smiled, warmer and wider than she had thought possible. The room seemed less cold. Amit stood, gesturing gently to Karan in the bed as he did so.

'That was what I'd hoped you'd say. I'll leave you two alone, then. Milli, he'll be confused when he wakes up. Help him through it.'

'I will,' she said and she knew that she meant it. Life with Karan might be hard, but life without him, now that she had seen him, would be impossible. As Amit left the room, Milli allowed herself to move her chair closer to the bed.

He was beautiful in his sleep, and he would be even more beautiful when he woke. She smoothed his hair, smiling as he murmured in his sleep. She took his hand in hers. She picked up a novel from his bedside table with her other hand and flipped it open. She wanted him to feel comforted and loved when he woke. She began to read aloud to him.

His hand tightened in her grip. She held him, safe and close which almost made her forget about her impending mortgage, her ailing mother and her miserable life so far.

TWELVE

When Karan regained consciousness, his first thought was that he must have died. As far as he could tell, he was in heaven. Everything around him was bathed in a fuzzy, golden light. The room was warm and peaceful, full of late afternoon sunlight. A sense of comfort and safety wrapped around Karan like a blanket, holding him tight. There was a low, pleasant murmuring of a woman's sweet voice in the background, and a soft hand holding his. The sensation soothed him and brought him back to earth. He tightened his grip around the hand as he blinked awake, struggling against the tendrils of sleep that held him fast to the bed. The world shimmied back into gentle focus.

He couldn't be in heaven because when his eyes opened, they opened to the same view he had been staring at for weeks: the full-length mirror above his bed. He heard a soft gasp from the chair at his bedside. It wasn't Amit. It was a woman. His mind swam uncomprehendingly as he tried to turn his head to see who it was holding his hand in hers. His heart leapt with joy when he realized with a jolt that the curls of soft dark hair falling across his chest as the woman leaned in close could only belong to one woman. *Milli.*

She was more beautiful in person. All curly dark hair, sun kissed skin and bright eyes the colour of tree moss, a pretty sundress wrapped around a curvy figure. Even her picture could not have prepared Karan for the grace she possessed as she moved, the sweetness of her smile, the generous, soft curves of her body as she leaned in close. The phone had masked the throaty hum of her voice as she spoke, soft and sweet. 'Karan?' she asked, 'are you awake?'

The sweetness of her voice muffled everything else around Karan – the numb pain in his head and the beeping of the monitors hooked up to his body. Nothing seemed to hurt with Milli by his side. She was better than morphine, she was a world without pain. Even trapped in this room that had become his hell, he felt as though he had been rescued and freed by Milli's presence. His eyes met Milli's and he gave her a weak smile, which was all he could muster.

'Milli,' he whispered. His throat was sore, his voice hoarse from disuse. But her name on his lips was the sweetest thing he had ever tasted and her answering smile lit up the room like a sunrise. His world was brighter with Milli in it.

'I'm here. I'm here,' she soothed, running a cool hand across his brow. The concern in her face was evident. 'What can I do to help?'

His body was overwhelmed with exhaustion. Just the effort of turning to admire her had worn him out. 'Keep reading,' he whispered, letting his eyelids droop. Milli's warm voice washed over him like a soft rainfall.

When he woke again, a few hours later, it was to his own words in her voice. While he'd been asleep, he had switched to a book he recognized as his second published volume of poetry. He couldn't help but smile at how fate had made her pick the particular volume.

Unlike his first, which had been an exploration of ennui, without much personal connection to Karan's life, or his third, which was a study in the terror of undergoing surgery, his second was a book of his hopes and dreams. Letters to a future lover, a wife he was yet to meet, the children she was yet to bear for them.

It was his happily ever after, one he imagined when he believed he might never feel happiness again. It was a pipe dream, a desperate plea for love written in a dark time of his life when he thought he might never see one.

But in Milli's voice, it didn't sound like a fantasy. It sounded like a future.

'Dark clouds converge overhead, warning erosion, threatening to drown all we love. But you, my promise of sunshine, you keep me afloat,' she read, her voice heavy with emotion. Her hands trembled on the page and she swallowed.

'You teach me to swim,' Karan finished, knowing the verse by heart. It was his favourite poem that he had ever written. 'God's promise of mercy in you, my rainbow…With you, my angel, I learn to fly without wings.'

Milli's eyes widened in surprise as she set the book down against the arm of the chair. Her green eyes were bright with tears. 'Karan,' she breathed. It sounded like a benediction.

'You like my poetry?' he asked. He couldn't keep the wonder out of his voice. She nodded, smiling.

'It's incredible. So eloquent. The girl you wrote this book for must have been very lucky. She was a fool to let you get away,' Milli blushed at her own boldness, but it made Karan laugh. He thought about Prachi, who had slipped through his fingers as easily as water, who had never opened one of his books and dismissed poetry as overly sentimental and self-congratulatory. She was nothing like Milli.

'I wrote the poems for someone I hadn't met yet,' he confessed. 'And most of the girls I've met since writing it didn't care to read my poetry. They only found poetry in the things they'd purchased with my credit cards,' he said with a weak smile. 'I've been waiting ever since I wrote them for someone like you to come along.'

'I love poetry,' Milli said, 'but yours might be my favourite. It feels personal to me. Like a song someone's been singing for my ears alone,' she bit her lip, too shy to continue. The trembling in her voice suggested she might cry. 'I thought you'd never wake up!' she said finally, sternly, to camouflage her anxiety. He admired her courage in the situation. He didn't know whether he could have stayed as strong as she did if their positions were to be reversed. Gazing down at him, there was no pity in her eyes: only love.

'I don't think I could sleep any longer. Your pretty face makes it hard to close my eyes. I never thought I'd see you. Not in this place,' he gestured weakly to the machinery around him, monitoring his recovery, keeping him alive and free from pain.

'You've got Amit to thank for that,' she said wryly. Karan cocked an eyebrow.

'Meddling old man,' he said with a laugh. There was a cup of coffee on the nightstand, mostly finished. The cream in it, which neither he nor Amit drank, suggesting that Amit had brought it up for Milli. The butler in question was nowhere to be seen, wisely giving them the space they needed. He had never been more grateful to Amit for his care, his support, his love. Without Amit, he wouldn't have Milli here with him with her hand in his.

'I don't mind his meddling, really,' Milli replied, 'I've missed you for what feels like my entire life. Being with you, in person, is the most incredible thing I've ever felt. I can leave if you want me to—'

'Never,' Karan reassured her quickly, 'I never want you to leave.'

'Good,' Milli sighed, 'because I don't want to leave either.'

With that she set the book on the nightstand, leaning in closer and closer still until she blurred in his vision. She smelled like sunlight and freshly cut herbs. When she kissed him, her mouth against his felt like dawn breaking across the darkest night. He was home in her arms as she wrapped them around his shoulders.

Milli's kiss sent a wave of electricity through Karan. Her soft lips against his, so sweet and careful as she kissed him, drove him wild. He felt healed, whole, and alive under her touch. It was so good it was almost too much. Her mouth was warm and inviting.

Finally, she pulled away, breathing hard. There was pain in Karan's body threatening to overtake him but Milli's happy face, flushed and smiling, numbed that feeling.

And as experienced as Karan was with women, nothing prepared him for the way he felt at this moment. Nothing he had ever felt before even came close to the feeling of Milli's lips on his. He wanted to drown in the lavender scent of her hair. He wanted to press himself so close to her sweet skin that he couldn't tell where he ended and she began. He wanted to know everything about her. How she looked when she slept, the peaceful expression on her face and the steady rise and fall of her chest.

Everything he saw with Milli in his fantasies was now a possible future. All he wondered about, all he dreamed about was Milli by his side. He hadn't been able to see a future at all before he saw her sitting in the chair across from his bed. But now, he could hope for the future. A good future, one in which he was healthy, growing old with the love of his life. All of this was possible only because she was with him. For the first time in weeks, Karan didn't have to fake a smile or any laughter. His joy was real.

Milli lay next to him on the bed, her hand tangled with his as she confessed in a whisper that he was more than she had ever dreamed about. That he made her happier than she had ever felt before. She traced the pattern of his scars with a reverent, careful hand, a look of wonder on her face. It confused him so to know that she wasn't repulsed by his innumerable scars. Instead, she told him that she thought they were battle wounds, they told the story of his battles. 'You've fought much harder than most of us will ever have to fight in our lives,' she told him, 'why shouldn't you wear them with pride?'

Karan's eyes welled with tears as she placed a sweet kiss on the scar tissue on his chest, looking up at him. There was a kindness and a love there that was alien to Karan. Most women made him feel like a monster or an invalid. For so long he believed himself to be damaged goods, a ruined freak, a waste of a man. An accident in survival, too cursed to ever be truly whole or truly loved.

She knew him fully now and it hadn't frightened her in the slightest. She was braver than he had imagined she could be. Now that he had her, he regretted the time he had spent without her. If only he had been a little braver, she could have been here all along, lying by his side.

She confessed other things to him, frightening, wonderful things. That she understood he couldn't walk. That she would be his legs, his guiding force. That she would be there for any surgery he needed. That it wouldn't frighten her off. 'I think I've waited for you all my life,' she said, 'and it's been hell without you by my side. D'you think these silly little added difficulties are going to frighten me off, after I've finally found you? Think again,' she whispered, pressing a kiss to his cheek.

And for the first time in his life, Karan believed someone wholeheartedly. It felt almost childish, to expect the best from anyone or any situation. Karan was a stranger to good luck. He feared that he had wasted all his luck on surviving his life so far. But then Milli came along and taught Karan how to hope. She was eternally optimistic. He felt as though her love might just be what the doctor ordered.

And when she smiled, he was certain she was the panacea he longed for his entire life.

They talked about everything and nothing together. Karan could forget all about his pain with Milli in his arms. They talked long into the afternoon about Karan's fears and Milli's dreams, about their shared difficulties in following literature from the American Romantic period and about Walt Whitman's lush language. They snuggled close together, wrapped up in silk sheets, her head on his chest, his mouth against her hair, her laughter in his ear, his hand in her hand.

When they couldn't think of anything else to say they communicated with kisses, filling the silence with lips pressed together, quiet laughter and whispered nothings. How funny that 'I love you' seemed too hard to say at full volume, when they were essentially promising each other a forever with touches and smiles. But Karan wasn't worried. It seemed as they lay in the bed together, Karan's body pressed close to Milli's, that they had all the time in the world.

Thirteen

Milli woke from a late afternoon dream to a hesitant knock on the door. For a moment, she thought that her mother had come back and was there to make some demand of her, but then her eyes opened to an opulent bedroom and the beep of medical equipment and she realized she had awakened far away from the world she knew. A sense of peace washed over her, even as her mind oriented itself to her unfamiliar surroundings. Had she ever slept so easily in her life as she did here, in this place where she had never been before? How could this house that was not hers, already feel like home?

Beside her, the answer snored lightly, almost but not quite stirring at the sound of the knock on the door. When it came once more, he let out a yawn and his coffee-coloured eyes snapped open. 'I'm up, Amit, I'm up,' he grumbled. Then he noticed Milli beside him. His whole demeanour underwent a change instantly. The same wonder she felt spread across his face. 'Milli,' he breathed.

'Good morning,' she greeted him with a sleepy smile.

'Good afternoon, I think,' he replied, and pressed his lips to hers. 'Possibly even good evening.'

'Karan,' came Amit's voice through the door, 'I just bought some groceries for you and your guest. I thought you'd want to offer her something more impressive than takeout.'

Milli thought she might have imagined the blush on Karan's face, but he seemed pleased enough. 'Thank you, Amit,' he said. To Milli he added, 'it sounds like we'll have something fresh for supper, after all. I'm grateful. Amit's left me to do most of the cooking since I was a child, as it was a hobby that I thoroughly enjoyed. He's never had much passion for it himself. So, during long stretches of illness like this, he brings home a lot of takeout. He claims that if I can't enjoy the usual master chef of this house, imported will have to do.'

He laughed and Milli tried to laugh with him, the joke was one she could only partially understand. If she was hungry she had to cook for herself. She had never considered it fun nor did she know any other means to get food into her belly. The meagre finances of her household proscribed fine things like dining out or the luxury of someone else doing the cooking for her. For Milli, cooking was just another thing to check off the to-do list and nothing more.

However, things had been different in Karan's case. She felt her heart fill with warm fondness, just thinking of the time he texted her cooking instructions while he was in Paris. It wasn't just anyone who would have considered it fun, much less a romantic gesture, to teach her to make frittata. But he had gone through the instructions step-by-step, as patient as a teacher, cheerleading her through the difficult preparation, and the results had been wonderful. The meal had been incredibly delicious, not just for the flavours but for the obvious care that Karan had taken to make sure that the food she ate was delicious and not merely nutritious. That it fed her soul and not only her body.

Slowly but surely, Milli was beginning to understand Karan. The experiences he saw as a luxury had little to do with the cost involved. Instead, the real value was its worth to the person who consumed it.

How cruel was it that this experience was currently out of his reach? Karan could barely go to the toilet without assistance in his injured state. Cooking a full meal, the sort he seemed to love from their many chats together, was certainly beyond him at this point in time. Milli wondered what they would do – it was possible that Amit would put together whatever Karan's favourite meal was for him, but Karan had just mentioned that Amit had no passion for cooking. Milli didn't have much passion for cooking either but she did have a passion for Karan. And so she would learn to love to cook on the off chance it might make Karan smile.

'I'll make supper tonight,' she blurted.

Karan looked at her strangely. 'I'm sure that Amit can manage, if you—' he began.

'I don't want Amit to manage. You love to cook and I'd love to learn. So, teach me. Let me be your hands. We'll cook a meal together. That's what I'd like, if you'll let me.'

She was aware she was being very bold for someone who was essentially just a guest in his house, a stranger whom he had not met until very, very recently. But, she felt a strange sense of peace in his home, as though it were hers, too. She supposed it was because the man who was, in some ways, her heart, resided here. And Karan had once enjoyed teaching her, before this accident. She only hoped that his unfortunate circumstances hadn't dampened his zeal for life. It didn't seem so, from the way they had talked.

For short periods of time, she could forget that he was even in a hospital bed. Because he was so animated with his words and articulate, it seemed his whole body was perfectly whole and healthy. She could tune out the sound of monitors for hours at a time, just listening to him speak. There was some sort of energy within him that the pain couldn't quench. He was funny, optimistic in spite of himself, and full of infectious joy that Milli relished. He grew tired more quickly than someone who's healthy, but he seemed practised enough at hiding that exhaustion.

Why frown when you could smile? That seemed to be his outlook on life. Even if you had very little to smile about, as Karan did, he smiled anyway. Each smile was a gift, because he was under no obligation to give it. And Milli received each one with pleasure.

'I'll have Amit help me downstairs,' Karan told her. 'You meet me down in the kitchen.'

'I'm afraid you'll have to direct me to the kitchen. I'm a little new to this particular village contained under a single roof,' she joked.

'With how long this recovery time might take me, I'm petitioning to have a subway system installed,' Karan grumbled. 'No word from the city planner yet, but believe me, with all this time I've got to spend in bed, I've plenty of time to call and pester him.'

'I'm only half certain you're joking,' Milli called over her shoulder, easing open the door.

Amit was standing on the other side, trying not to look amused. 'The main hallway by the stairs will take you to almost any room in the house that is currently in use. When the whole of the Singhania family was in residence, the rooms in the other wing were a flurry of activity and the second kitchen was often in use. They're a family that loves to cook. But now that it's only Karan and I, only one of the kitchens, the library, the master suite, and my quarters are currently occupied.'

'Thank you,' Milli said earnestly. 'Truly. For all of this. For everything.'

'It was no trouble, Milli,' Amit replied. 'I'm the one who should be thanking you. From the way I've seen him light up since he found you in his room, I think you truly are saving his life.'

Milli wasn't sure what to say to that. It was hard to find the words to voice her thoughts. In reality, she and Karan were saving each other. Life with him had purpose. With his hand in hers, Milli could see freedom within her grasp. She just had to find her mother and regain her balance in this ever-whirling world. But all that could wait after dinner.

———•———

Milli's first observation upon reaching the kitchen after a long trek through the winding hallway, was that the kitchen had more counter space than her entire house. In fact, the kitchen seemed almost as big as the entire first floor of her home. More than that, it seemed that all of its contents were arranged purposefully, placed intricately, as though someone had simply imported the contents of a catalogue into a home. There was no clutter the way they was in Milli's cluttered kitchen: the kitchen had exactly what it needed, and nothing more. Each sparkling tool was expensive and well-maintained, although Milli could tell that they had been well used.

The kitchen was clean and airy, full of sunlight. Its wide windows let Milli see a beautiful view of the lake, the swans swimming at sunset. Milli gained a sense that the kitchen was an oasis for Karan's family. With the care the room was shown, you could see just how valued the room was to them.

Milli was no expert chef, so she was relying on Karan to assist her in every way that mattered. Between the refrigerator and the pantry, the potential for a great curry blossomed before her eyes. That thought was confirmed by the only thing slightly out of place on the countertop: a plain three-ring binder, stained and frayed from years of use. The words *Family Recipes* were printed on its worn surface in a sharpie scrawl that might have been Karan's or, more likely, his mother's. She flipped through the book till she came across a food-splattered page clearly most loved by the Singhania family – a fairly simple recipe for a mutton curry.

'The mutton curry recipe on page thirty-seven in the family favourite,' Karan confirmed as Amit pushed him through the door in a wheelchair. Even though he seemed tired, his eyes lit up seeing Milli in the kitchen. It seemed to Milli that he saw what she saw: she belonged here, just like his family's recipe book and all the shining cooking implements that were stocked in the kitchen. It was strange, Milli thought, to belong to such opulence when she had never touched things as grand as these in her life. But she did. Because she belonged with Karan.

'Where do we begin?' she asked, ready to get down to work.

Soon, the clean kitchen was full of the sound of bubbling oil and the sweet, rich smell of onions frying in the pan. Milli put a generous dollop of garlic ginger paste into the pan and stirred it into the frying onions. She leaned a little too close to enjoy the scent, but backed away hurriedly when the oil popped.

'We wouldn't want to scar your pretty face!' Karan laughed as she defensively hopped away from the wok. He was seated by the island, watching her work with a lot of pride and a little envy in his expression. 'You'll probably want to add the mutton pieces to the mix soon,' he added, watching the pan keenly, 'brown them and then we'll add in the rest of the spices.'

In a little bowl by the pan, Milli stirred together some salt, red chilli powder, turmeric, powdered coriander and cumin seeds which she sprinkled into the pan, coating the browned mutton, letting the intoxicating scent of a good curry fill her nostrils. She ran an idle finger through the remaining traces of the powdered mix in the bowl, then placed it to her tongue.

'Mmm,' she hummed. She could understand just how the spices would blend with the garlic, ginger and onion to flavour the mutton richly. Of course it was a family favourite.

She picked up a sharp ceramic knife and sliced into a rich round tomato, enjoying the scent that wafted from it as she diced it into small pieces. She worked slowly and a little clumsily with the knife, but there was a meditative quality to the cooking that she found she enjoyed, especially when she thought about the day Karan would cook for her. She supposed in a way he was, by showing her the recipe that was clearly a family treasure. She didn't think he would do this for just any girl. She adding the tomatoes into the curry, giving it a little stir to mix them in properly.

'The curd is in the refrigerator, when you need it. I'd go ahead and start the rice cooker about now as well, if I were you,' Karan said, interrupting her thoughts. 'It smells incredible, by the way. I'm reminded of my own cooking, smelling the wonderful food you're making. I know you don't think so, but you're a natural. We'll make a chef of you.'

The encouragement made Milli blush as she reached into the refrigerator for the curd. The creamy factor it would give the curry would round the flavours and turn good into incredible. She couldn't help but think that Karan might be right about that, but if she hadn't had his encouragement, she would have never learned this about herself. They strengthened each other. It was a nobel feeling.

As the curry simmered, Milli started turning on the rice cooker and set out three plates and cups for supper.

'Amit won't be joining us for supper,' Karan told her, 'he told me that he wouldn't dream of interrupting us and would much rather have the leftovers when we were done.'

Milli would miss Amit, whom she was growing to like, but she had to admit that she was grateful not to have a chaperone for her first meal with Karan. As the rice cooker clicked off, Milli trimmed a little coriander off the plant growing in the sunlight of the window to use as a garnish. She plated the curry, pouring it over the rice, then garnished it with delight, smiling at Karan who smiled back. It wasn't as pretty as a chef might have done, but she was certain it would taste wonderful.

'Looks incredible,' Karan told her as she wheeled his wheelchair to the kitchen table. 'I usually eat in here when I'm well and it's just Amit and me,' he added as she filled his glass with chardonnay. 'When I was a child we would host many dinners as beautiful as this one in the formal dining hall, but we haven't had visitors like that since my parents left for Europe.'

The thought of being in the large dining hall scared her somewhat. She barely knew the difference between a salad fork and an entrée fork, although an advice column she had scanned during a lull at the airport's duty-free counter, had told her where she could find them located in a formal dining setting. Still, a fork was a fork to Milli. Not a single piece of her silverware was actual silver, unlike the fork she was currently holding.

'I'd like that too,' Karan smiled at her. Then he lifted the fork to his lips. His expression was one of rapture. 'Oh, Milli!' he exclaimed. 'You have no idea how good this tastes after weeks of takeout, and worse, hospital food.'

Milli exaggerated a shudder. 'Hospital food, God forbid!' she muttered, then took a bite of the curry.

She couldn't believe it was something she had made. Generally, even the cereal she made for herself tasted mediocre because of her apathy towards its preparation. But this meal, in which she had truly invested herself, was even better than the frittata she had made before. 'Keep teaching me how to cook like this and I'll stay forever,' she told Karan, blushing as soon as she had spoken. Her boldness around him embarrassed her. But Karan didn't reply. He was too busy enjoying the meal. They descended into grunts of pleasure and companionable silence.

———•———

Karan scraped his plate, then scraped it again, although there was nothing left on it but traces of the gravy. Milli was just about to offer to serve him seconds when he glanced up. The vestiges of his enjoyment of the meal they had just shared were replaced by something akin to desperation in his eyes. He reached out and she took his hand in hers, suddenly worried that he might be in pain. 'I don't want to go back up to that prison of a bedroom just yet,' he said. 'Please, Milli, let's stay downstairs just a moment longer. Wheel me into the library. It's just down the hall from here. I would love nothing more than the sight of you surrounded by my books, my most precious one standing there amongst my precious things.'

'Of course,' Milli agreed instantly, her face flushing at the compliment, although her concern hadn't lessened any. She left the plates on the table, planning to deal with them just as soon as she figured out how to wash such fine china and silver. She wheeled him into a massive room that was covered with books, everything from encyclopaedias to textbooks of economics to poetry to paperback romances. She was almost offended that she hadn't been given a tour of this room yet. Surely, Karan would have known that this room would be her favourite in the house, just as it was his.

He did seem happier in here, just as she was, although there was still the slightest hint of sadness in his coffee dark eyes that nothing she did seemed to erase. It was fair, even on such a happy day, to expect some melancholy from Karan. Especially after everything he had been through.

She realized that in his own way, Karan was in a lot more pain than she could ever understand, the sort that no medication could cure. Trapped in a body that should have been in its prime, running wild and free, instead he could do little more than raise his head off the bed. He still had the dignity of being able to feed himself, to move in short bursts from room to room, although it was clear that the effort exhausted him like a full day of work might exhaust Milli. But he didn't have the ability of moving like a man, of literally sweeping her off her feet, of stealing her away and making love to her all night long the way she wanted him to do.

Still, she could make him feel like a king just by standing at his side. She could inspire him and strengthen him where he felt weak, like only his queen could. She was his heart. She had to be strong for him. Milli put on her prettiest smile for him, standing there amongst his books, the golden light of the study haloing her. She looked like an angel to him, the way his eyes lit up, dispelling all that dark sadness that had dulled them. They were electric, coffee black eyes. His hungry gaze sent a jolt through her. She wanted him. She wanted to do something for him that would make sure he never forgot her. That whenever he heard music, he thought of her in this way. His angel from heaven to bring him joy in his darkest hour.

'Play me your favourite song,' she said. A smile spread across his face at that. This was something they hadn't shared yet. Something that had the potential to be wonderful.

Karan flipped a switch and music filled the room through an incredible surround-sound system. Milli could feel the notes, crisp and clear, in her bones. The violin came in softly, the music surrounded her all at once like a flock of butterflies rising from a field. It crescendoed above her, warm and romantic, the piano following its pattern upwards, sounding as lovely as a child's laugh. There was wonder rumbling deep in the bass notes of the song and the cello promised delight, luxury and decadence in its vibrato.

'Dance for me, Milli,' Karan said, even as she felt her body begin to move to the undeniable sway of the song.

There was something about moving for someone, at their request and for their pleasure, that felt more intimate than taking your clothes off could ever be. Milli felt a heaviness, an awkwardness to her movements that usually a partner could lift, with his firm hands on her waist, guiding her to where she needed to be. But that was not an option now. Karan simply wasn't strong enough, although he looked at her with such a strange expression on his face that she thought he could hold her up with just the force of his love.

She spun around on her heels like a child, laughing as she made up moves, treading the line between sensuous and silly. She had never been much of a dancer but had always liked the way her body felt in motion, playing with rhythm and melody, exploring the music. She had always longed for the freedom she had heard that girls her age were supposed to have, dancing in clubs all night with their best friends. Dancing reminded her of a good and different life.

She let her hands shape the sounds they heard as she spun around in circles, a little dizzy with the love she felt. She let out a laugh, a sound that was pure light and freedom bubbling forth from her chest. She couldn't remember the last time she had felt this happy, but here in this strange new place where she couldn't help but feel she belonged. All the weight was off her shoulders when she heard Karan laugh. He was watching her as though he had never seen anything more beautiful in his life, as though in his world of luxuries and endless pretty things she was the finest thing he had.

She supposed in some way, that was true. Had she ever felt so wonderful in her life as she did in this moment, revelling in a lover's smile and appreciative gaze? There was no glittering gold jewellery, no fast sports car or bottle of sparkling champagne that could match the thrill of discovering the way they felt about each other. Having someone who loved you totally, holding their heart in your hand, meant more than anything your wealth could buy you.

As the song swelled to a thundering crescendo, Milli let herself imagine making a life of the love she had found here with Karan.

She wanted to build a home within this haunted house, restoring the love evident on its rooms. This was the life she wanted: crafting a loving family for Karan and building back the protective walls his family had made around his heart when he was just a child. It would start small, with smiles and dancing after dinner, flowers in vases and home-cooked meals. One day, she would look up and everything she wanted would be at her fingertips. And on that day, Karan would pull her into his strong arms and ask her to dance for him once more.

This was their life, she realized. Not a prequel, not a rehearsal. Their future together had already begun. The things they did together now made a foundation for a lifetime of happiness or sadness. It was their choice whether or not to celebrate each victory in their lives, no matter how much pain existed alongside that joy. Dancing for Karan wasn't a flirtation – it was a celebration. It was a firm step forwards towards victory, a step into the sunlight, a step towards love.

Milli shook out her hair, letting it cascade down her back. With a wild spin, she sent a dark halo of curls flying around her head, spreading out like the sun's rays throughout the room. The song dipped a little, preparing to build up to its climax. She tossed a look back at Karan over her shoulder, aiming for sultry but hitting him with a bright beam of open affection instead. He returned it in kind.

Milli noticed his hands twitching, as though he wanted nothing more than to take her into his arms. So as the song settled, its last notes rising like a firework and then fizzling out as fast, she settled at his side, a little out of breath.

'Hi,' she breathed, a smile spreading across her face.

'Hi,' he replied, and leaned in to kiss her.

His kisses were as sweet as heaven on her lips. What Milli wouldn't give to live in a world that began and ended with his lips against hers...she could kiss him for hours, enjoying nothing more than the sensations he sent through her body with every touch of his skin. She could lose herself in the feeling of his fingers pressing hesitantly, then more insistently at her back, as he learned the curves of her body. Karan was an incredible kisser, someone who knew how to speak through his hands and mouth without saying a word. With every touch of his lips against hers, Milli understood how much he wanted her, how happy he was to be holding her, how intoxicated he was with her scent, her touch, her very being. That intoxication was mutual.

Kissing was a doorway to a world that was entirely their own. In that strange and wonderful universe, they became KaranandMilli, a wild bundle of nerves and veins that came alive in every spot they connected. Every place their skin touched lit up like an electrical bulb. The sound of heavy breaths and moans filled the air as the kiss deepened. Time no longer existed as a linear path for them to follow. There was only this moment, which might have been the next, which might have been the one before. Each one was a moment of ecstasy.

Until the moment came crashing down around their heads with the sound of a gentle cough from the doorway. They sprang apart like teenagers, guilty of being caught. Milli could feel her blush all the way from her cheeks to her toes as Amit let himself into the room, looking, if possible, even more embarrassed.

'I, um,' Amit struggled, seemingly at a loss for words. 'I wanted to offer to do the washing up. I assumed you must be tired by now, Karan. I see that I was, er … wrong about that,' he began to back away hastily. 'Really, it's no trouble for me to wash the dishes. Let me know if you need my help getting up the stairs to bed.'

'Goodnight, Amit!' Karan called to him, still blushing.

'Goodnight!' Amit called through the closed door. Karan and Milli found themselves sitting far apart, at each end of the couch.

They looked at each other for a moment. Then Karan burst out laughing.

'Your face, your face,' he cackled, turning red this time not from embarrassment, but from breathlessness caused by laughter.

'Your face!' Milli retorted through her own laughter. Her ribs hurt and her smile was so wide she thought it might crack her face open. 'The man is like a father to you, I thought when he opened the door you were going to have a cute mini panic attack—"

"You blanched like a child caught with her hand in the cookie jar!" he howled.

"Think about how poor Amit must have felt!" And that set them both off again, clutching each other with laughter. Tears rolled down Karan's face. Milli could tell that it was exhausting him, but she had heard that laughter really was the best medicine, and it seemed to do him good to be out of the bedroom. Milli wasn't a healer by nature. She usually found herself waiting around until life could really begin, hoping to find her true purpose down the road, maintaining the life that she could and dreaming of nothing more than a weekend of rest and a hot meal for supper. But, with Karan, she felt for the first time, a purpose beyond keeping herself alive. With him, she felt like a person who was complete.

She collapsed on the couch, resting her head by Karan's lap from where she could look up at his face. He was lovely like this, lovely from every angle, just as handsome with a goofy grin on his face as he was with the serious, pondering expression he often wore when he thought Milli wasn't looking. He carded his fingers absently through her long hair, enjoying the softness of it, the scent of her shampoo. A moment later, she felt gentle tugging at her hair.

'My sister bullied me into learning to braid her hair when we were children,' he explained, weaving strands of her hair together into a tight, thin braid. 'I thought it was silly at first, but there's a real meditative quality in using your hands that way. She's been gone for years now, lives in Europe with the rest of my family and I've never been much for growing out my hair,' Milli let out a snort at the thought of him with long, braided hippie hair. 'So I haven't had anyone to practise on in a while.'

'I don't mind if you play with my hair,' she said, 'honestly, most girls I know would kill for a boyfriend who could braid hair.' When she realized the word she had just used, she blushed deeper than she had when Amit had caught them making out like teenagers on the couch. Karan wouldn't let it slide, though. Of course, he wouldn't.

'Boyfriend, huh?' he asked. Milli pulled a curtain of hair across her face and let out a groan.

'Or, you know, I mean ...' she trailed off.

'No, I like it. I'd like that. To be your boyfriend.' Milli gazed up at him. It was like staring into the sun, watching him smile so radiantly.

'I'd like that, too,' she agreed. It was all she could say. She shifted upwards to where his lips were waiting and captured him in a kiss. Another kiss and they were catapulting back into their own universe, all too willing to lose themselves in each other once more.

FOURTEEN

Sunlight streamed through the window, bathing the room in the light of a gorgeous summer morning. A ray fell across Milli's face, warming her skin. She yawned and stretched, turning towards it. She pushed the silk sheets covering her body to the side, blinking awake wearily. Karan was lying by her side, face still relaxed in sleep as he breathed deeply. He looked better, somehow, than when she had first seen him in the bed. He had looked so small and tired then, as though he had been broken beyond repair. Now he looked more whole, as though he were healing faster with his hand in hers.

It was amazing, Milli thought, what hope could do to a man. Through his loneliness and his suffering, Karan had almost lost what made him most incredible to Milli – his hope. But she had seen it rekindle in his eyes when he first saw her, and it seemed to strengthen him even as he slept to hold her hand in his. *How incredible to be with him,* she thought. *To have held him all night long. His hand in mine. This man. My man.*

It didn't seem at all strange to Milli to finally be with him. She had thought, before they had met, that they might not have the same chemistry when they were face to face. And it was true, in a way. Apart, they had been infatuated with each other, talking at all hours of the day and night. But now, they needed no longer needed words to show each other how they felt. He held her hand.

He whispered in her ear. He made her smile like no man ever had. There was time when she had worried that she might fall for him and now she felt no fear. She had fallen and it had taken her to new heights unlike anything she had ever felt before. Even balanced perilously on the edge of the bed with nothing but the sound of Karan's steady breathing to lull her to sleep, she felt more rested than she had felt in years of sleeping in her own bed.

It was all Karan; his presence, having him within arms' reach when she had wanted nothing more than to hold him for so long. Milli had never felt so much at peace, so close to home, as she did with Karan by her side. Her future was before her. Her happiness was guaranteed. Even through the suffering that would befall Karan before he could walk again, his surgeries and therapies and the slow, crushing weight of time, she would hold him up. They would hold each other.

His face was beautiful in sleep. His chiselled jawline, his dark, curling hair a mess on his pillow, his well shaped, firm lips slightly parted as he inhaled deeply. She couldn't help pressing a kiss, as gently as she could, to his lips. With a start, he opened his eyes, blinking away the remains of his dream. He was so much better than anything she had dreamed that night. Karan, Karan. He owned her heart and he hadn't even had to ask for it. She was eternally his.

'G'morning, beautiful,' he said, his voice husky with sleep. He looked stronger today. Healthier. Happier. Already she could tell it was going to be a beautiful day. With him by her side, how could it not be?

'G'morning, handsome,' she whispered, leaning in for a kiss. He met her mouth joyfully, still sleepy as he kissed her. His kisses increased in passion as he slowly came back into the waking world.

They might have kissed for what might have been minutes or hours. It was so easy to lose track of time when Karan's lips were on hers and his hand was tangled in her hair. It was nearly impossible to keep her hands off him for any amount of time now that she had a taste of what he promised her with every press of his mouth to hers. She wanted nothing more than to keep kissing him for the rest of their lives. His lips were addictive.

Even with the smell of medicine permeating his skin, the underlying sweet scent in the stale room that was all Karan intoxicated her and drove her wild. It was easy to ignore the weakness in his muscles and, indeed, the whole impossibility of their current situation in favour of kissing him again when his mouth against hers felt so right. His smile against her mouth made her crave more and more. And when he whispered her name in her ear she gave a full body shiver, completely beside herself with how much her skin craved his. She wanted him badly and she could tell that he wanted her, too. But with his condition, she wasn't sure that she could.

Unfortunately, or fortunately, before Milli could figure out just what she could do to him, they were interrupted mid-kiss by the sound of Milli's alarm blaring loudly from the nightstand, making her groan with annoyance. However, before she could deal with it, Karan's hand reached out from under the sheets and hit the snooze button. 'Forget that thing,' he said, 'and come back here to me.' He held her in a grip that must have used up most of his strength, embracing her fully. The feeling of his skin against hers held her entranced. If she had wanted to struggle, she could get away, but with his body so close to hers, the last thing she wanted to do was to leave.

'Karan,' she groaned, laughing as he pressed kisses to her neck, 'the alarm means I have to leave. I've got to go to work. You can't just—' she chuckled as he started to tickle her ribs.

'You were saying?' he teased, poking her side with his index finger. She giggled, and started to push him away. He relented and loosened his arms from around her.

'Work. I was saying work.' she admonished him, extricating herself from his arms. He propped himself up against the headboard in a slow, deliberate motion, studying her as she rushed about the room, getting her things together. She felt so conflicted about leaving him but knew she had to do it if she was going to save her home. 'Work means making money. Money means fixing this stupid house payment issue. Fixing the stupid house payment issue means I get to come here and crawl right back into bed with you, which is all I really want to do.'

He was amused by the domino reasoning, stretching luxuriously as she fumbled beneath the nightstand for her phone charger. He watched her with starving eyes, following the movement of her body like he wanted nothing more than to hop up and join her, or to drag her back into bed with him. She wanted nothing more than to crawl back into his arms and fall asleep once more with her head pillowed against his strong shoulder. *Willpower,* she told herself, *willpower and hard work. That's how you'll fix your mother's problems. Then you'll be free to see Karan whenever you want. Then your life will finally be your own.*

'Alternate proposal for you,' he said with a winning smile.. 'Why don't we skip steps one and two. You play hooky from work and come back to bed. I give you the money to fix whatever problem you're talking about with your house and we'll make everything right without even having to put on pants or leave the room. Sounds good?'

Milli stiffened, bristling with hurt at Karan's careless words. She knew he meant it mostly as a joke. She knew that he was lonely and that by leaving him she was abandoning him to all the misery he had been suffering through these past few weeks. She knew that he understood how badly she wanted to stay with him and how bad she felt that she couldn't. But still, the offer of money, thrown so casually her way by someone who had always had it, did hurt her. Didn't he understand just how self-made and self-reliant she had always been? She had worked hard since she was a teenager to save for everything she had. She had very little, but what she did have hadn't come easily. She wasn't a charity case or a good time girl who could be bought for some lump sum. Maybe his previous girlfriends had been that sort, but Milli wasn't.

She could tell he was aware that he had put his foot in his mouth, but the damage was done. She quickly wound up her charger cable and tucked it into her purse. Luckily, she hadn't brought much so she could leave before the shame and humiliation she felt took its toll and she burst into tears.

'Milli,' he said, his quiet voice sweet as he reached for her. 'I'm sorry, I didn't mean to hurt you. I can see that you're upset. Talk to me, please?'

And that was why she had fallen for him in the first place. Her anger dissipated as quickly as it grew. He cared and he was trying. He didn't know everything that had happened to her to make her feel this way. And he was afraid of being left alone. He wanted her honesty, so she would give it to him.

'I'll be okay,' she said, 'but there are some things I need to figure out. My mother mortgaged our home without telling me and we might end up losing it. I have some savings put away, enough for them to hold out on foreclosure, but not enough to pay off what we owe – what she owes. She did this …,' she sighed, 'because she's an addict. Opiates, pills mostly. I think she lost her job. I know we're losing the house. So as much as I'd love to stay with you all day, I can't. I have to fix this. And I have to find her,' she said, slinging her purse over her shoulder.

'I understand,' he nodded. But she knew it was only so she wouldn't feel bad about leaving him behind for the day. Her face softened.

'I'll be back soon, Karan,' she said, 'so soon you won't even realize I've been gone. And I'll come right back to bed, and I'll read to you, and it'll be like I never left.'

'Sounds amazing,' he smiled.

'It will be.' She leaned in to press a kiss to his lips, then took another lingering kiss just because she could. *Karan. My man.* She thought. 'I'll be back here later this evening. It depends on how long it takes with the bank after my shift. I'll pick up a toothbrush, some pyjamas—'

'You won't need them,' he teased with a smirk.

'A few changes of clothes for the next couple of days,' she continued. 'But I'll be home to watch the sunset in your arms. Wait for me.'

'I don't have anywhere else to go, don't worry,' he indicated the bed. Milli blushed a little. She hadn't meant to make light of his situation. But he didn't seem overly bothered by the comment. She admired his sense of humour so. It was rather sexy to have a man by her side who could laugh with her even through the worst of situations.

'I have to go, Karan,' she said, reluctantly pulling out of his grasp as she fumbled for her car keys. Out his window she could see her sedan still parked in his driveway. He lived further away from the airport than she did. There was no way that she wouldn't be late, even if she left right now and sped down the highway. But it was okay. It had been worth it, all the trouble she would go through at work, to spend more time with Karan.

'Okay, okay,' he laughed, letting her go. She was almost in the hallway when she heard him take her name.

'Yes?' she asked, rushing back into the room, afraid he might be hurting.

'I didn't mean to insult you. I've just, I've never met a beautiful girl who wasn't using me for my money before,' he said. There was such honesty on his face that she couldn't help the adoration she felt towards him. They came from such different worlds but if they could bear that in mind and give each other grace, they might make it. And there was nothing Milli wanted more than to make things work with Karan.

'Hi,' she introduced herself, 'my name is Milli. And I love you just for who you are. Not your money. Not your scars. Not your books of poetry. Just that wonderful thing inside you that makes you…you,' she put her hand over her heart. Then before he could say another word, she ducked out the door and into the hallway. Yes, running late had been worth it, just to tell him that. She was in her car by the time she realized exactly what it was she had said to him.

Love, she thought. *I do. I love him.*

The thought made her heart light. She smiled for the entire drive to work. She couldn't wait to turn her car around and come back home. *Home,* she thought, for once not picturing her front porch. Instead, she saw the way Karan's face had split into a smile as she turned on her heel and walked out the door.

FIFTEEN

Milli's steps were light on the front porch. She could see the lights still glowing in the kitchen. Probably she forgot to turn them off when she left in a rush the previous day. She felt guilty for a moment about the waste before remembering that she was the one who paid the electricity bill. It was her prerogative to run that number up as she pleased. Her finances were ruined anyway, what was another few rupees added onto the electric bill?

The screen door creaked protestingly on its rusty springs as she pressed her shoulder into it and forced it open. *WD-40*, she thought. *And a toothbrush. And my toothpaste. Three sets of clothes. Underpants, obviously. My cutest bra. Some deodorant. Will I really need pyjamas?*

Her own thoughts made her blush. She thought of Karan's joke from earlier and flushed some more. She was so distracted that she tripped in the kitchen doorway and stumbled. That was when she saw something that made her heart lurch.

Her mother was passed out across the kitchen table, her pill bottle spilling from her hand. A dusting of blue pills and powder across the same wooden surface where Milli and her brother had often breakfasted together. A puddle of vomit in the exact spot that they would mix the batter for pancakes on Saturday mornings. The pale shell of a woman Milli's mother once was.

Milli's purse dropped to the floor. She rushed over to her mother, shaking her hard by the shoulder. 'Mama? Mama, please,' she yanked the woman up roughly, but her body flopped back to the table like a rag doll. She didn't stir. 'Mama, wake up, please,' Milli could feel the tears streaming down her face as her breath came in short gasps. *No,* was all she could think. *No, please, not like this.*

Finally, she had the presence of mind to check her mother's pulse. Slow, but still there. Her breathing was shallow and irregular but she was still breathing. There was still time. There was still hope.

The hospital bill is one you can't afford, for all the bells and whistles nonsense of trying to get an ambulance out here. Besides, chances are you'll be dead before they get out to the property, anyway. That was what Milli had always been told. But Milli knew time was of the essence. If the medical personnel didn't get on site and soon, Milli would lose her mother entirely. She couldn't let that happen.

So, she dialled three digits. 102. She noticed a text from Karan but her eyes blurred with tears and she couldn't read it. The phone call went through, ringing twice before the operator said, '102, what's your emergency?'

'It's my mother,' Milli said, hating the tremble in her voice. 'There's been an accident. Or ... I don't know. She overdosed. Please send help right away!' she rapidly recited her address and begged them to come quickly before she sank to her knees, trembling. She was blind with panic, deaf with fear. She wasn't sure how long she lay curled in the foetal position, sobbing. She might have called Karan's name as she heard the sirens wailing up the driveway. But by the time the ambulance lights flashed through the window, she had collected herself. She scooped the bottle of her mother's pills into a plastic baggie and presented them to the first Emergency Medical Technician who came through the door.

'I don't know if this is all she took. Please, you have to help her. She's been struggling for so long, I don't know what to do—'

'It's quite alright, ma'am. Please, stand back and let us do our job,' the woman said to her, passing the pills to her associate as she moved to examine Milli's mother.

'Vital signs weak and fading. Acute overdose. Get her on the stretcher,' the woman said. She began rattling off instructions to the other EMTs, something about 5cc's of this, 2cc's of that, stomach-pumping, and keeping her stable until they got her to the Emergency Room. The world blurred around Milli as though she was the one who had swallowed too many pills, everything going fuzzy and numb. She was in shock, she noted distantly, as though she were watching herself living through this on a TV screen instead of experiencing it in real life. *Someone get that girl a blanket, can't you see her heart is breaking and it's a potentially fatal situation?* The flashing lights of the ambulance nauseated her. She closed her eyes to them for just a moment, shutting everything out.

'Ma'am? Ma'am!' the EMT said in a brisk voice. The sharp sound, like a slap, pulled Milli straight back to reality. Her stomach gave an unpleasant jolt as she saw her mother in the stretcher, an oxygen mask across her face. 'There's room for one in the ambulance. I suggest you collect insurance cards, IDs and take them with you. Hurry, there's not much time!'

Milli bolted into action, dashing to her room and flipping through her underwear drawer for the medical cards. Luckily, her mother couldn't sell them for anything. Milli could tell her mother had torn up Milli's room in rage or desperation, looking for more money for more pills. But she couldn't care about that now. Sliding anything that looked remotely useful into her wallet, Milli ran for the door. Her mother was already loaded into the ambulance when she climbed into the back, a mess of wires, needles, and masks woven like a tapestry to somehow keep her alive.

Her hand twitched a little with every beep of the Electrocardiogram. Milli noticed something odd on her mother's hand. She had to lean in close before she could tell what it was. It was the engagement ring Rahull had tossed at her, too-tight to even slide all the way onto her mother's little finger, it was stuck above the knuckle. The only thing beautiful on her body anymore. Milli wasn't sure when her mother had pawned her own wedding ring for drugs, but it was long enough ago now that there wasn't even a tan mark to show where the ring had been.

It was never much of a commitment, Milli thought, *only married 'til a younger, prettier woman did tore them apart.* Nevertheless, her mother had kept the ring. Out of pride, out of vanity, out of a misguided belief that Milli's father would come back to them. By the time Milli had been old enough to ask, her mother was too drugged-up to remember.

How long has it been this bad? Milli wondered. *Before Karan reminded me what normal was, was I just too blind to see?*

Her mother's hand twitched again. Milli couldn't stand it. She clasped the cold hand in her own, trying to warm her as best she could.

Hold on, Milli thought. *Please, please just hold on.*

She wasn't sure whether she was thinking of her mother or of Karan.

———◦———

Karan's worry was turning from apprehension into fear. He knew she had gone back to her mother's house to gather some things before coming home, but the sun had long since set and there was still no sign of her. Karan was medically tired, the sort of haze from drugs and pain that would force his eyes to close and his body to hibernate. However, he kept his eyes peeled open and his mind focussed, waiting for Milli.

But Milli did not return.

He called once, then sent a text to let her know that he was thinking of her. When he got no response for half an hour he called again. He didn't like the way he was feeling. The anticipation and anxiety was getting the better of him. A foreboding spread across his body, hurting worse than the pain from his hips. His whole body was on high alert. His hair standing at the nape of his neck. He had never had his instincts telling him so clearly that something was horribly wrong. He called her again and again, dialling and re-dialling like a madman and not getting through even once.

Karan started contemplating over the fact that Milli lived a dangerous life, although she had grown like a daisy through the concrete above the horror of her family. Her mother was ill, sick and possibly even violent. Cruel when she was aware of her actions and clumsy to the point of destruction when she wasn't. There was a man, Rahull, who despite claiming to love her, had abandoned her to walk home alone along a deserted highway on a pitch-black Chandigarh night. She claimed he had a temper. What would he do if he found out she was in love with another man?

There were too many dangerous factors in Milli's life and Karan, miserable and bedridden as he was, could do nothing to protect her. What kind of man was he if he couldn't stand up and fight for her? All he could do was sit there, miserable and exhausted, pressing the call button over and over again on her phone and hoping that she would answer eventually, instead of the police.

A knock on the door broke Karan out of his brooding. 'Yes?' he called, 'come in, Amit!'

'Not your butler,' Dr Lox laughed, giving a mocking little bow as he entered. 'Just a friend, I'm afraid,' he frowned, immediately adopting the doctoral mode that reminded Karan he was dealing with one of the brightest medical minds in the nation. 'You're looking rough, Karan. What's wrong?'

'Nothing your medicine can fix, I'm afraid,' Karan muttered, examining his phone. Sixteen outgoing calls to Milli and no response. He had never done anything like this before, blowing up a woman's phone like this with numerous calls one after the other. But then he had never had this sinking feeling before, either. His whole nervous system felt as though it were on fire, an alarm shrieking *Something's wrong! Something's wrong!*

'My medicine might not be able to but that's why we're heading out to Chandigarh Hospital tonight. Your family is informed and they're flying over. They'll see you at the hospital. Dr Suresh Nathan flew in from Singapore two days ago and has been preparing for your surgery. He says he'll be ready for you tomorrow morning if we start the surgery prep soon,' announced Dr Lox, wholly oblivious to Karan's consternation. 'Amit packed your bags last night, so all that's left to do is get you out of this room and to Chandigarh Hospital.'

Karan gaped, aware that he looked crazy and not caring. 'I'm sorry, what?' he asked finally, his manners coming through for him when his mind could not. He scrambled for his phone and checked the date.

'The hip replacement we scheduled two months ago, Karan,' Dr Lox reminded him patiently, knowing that his most recent head injury had discombobulated him entirely. Milli hadn't helped matters either, giving him the most wonderful night of his life by just lying next to him in the bed and then disappearing with the sunrise. No wonder he was so confused. Time had shifted off its axis, befuddling Karan. Now it was all falling back into place, only for him to find he had run out of time.

But this wasn't Karan's first rodeo with surgery, and even if things went well, it wouldn't be his last. 'Alright, Doc,' he said, trying to harness his sense of humour and get a few more digs into Dr Lox before his operation, 'lead the way. But know that if I die, I'm getting buried in that Dolce and Gabbana suit. You're not getting it in my will.'

'What about your scarves?' Dr Lox teased. 'You won't need scarves if you die.'

'On the contrary,' Karan deadpanned, 'my body will be very cold if I die. I'll need every single one of them to warm me up.'

'Damn,' Dr Lox cursed, 'if you live, can I have them?'

'If I live, we can negotiate,' Karan said, 'maybe you'll trade me your Rolex?'

'Not in a million years,' Dr Lox assured him, 'not over my dead body, or yours, will you be getting my Rolex.'

Dr Lox and Amit together assisted him into his wheelchair. 'Not as dignified as your Porsche, old boy,' Lox teased him, 'but I'll pretend you're travelling in style if you will.'

Karan gave a laugh he didn't really feel and assured Dr Lox that he would. Amit gave his hand another tight squeeze.

'Your parents, your sister and I will be waiting for you at the hospital. They'll be so happy to see you, Karan. Just hold on to that thought until we get there,' he told Karan.

When they lifted him into the ambulance, pain jolted through his hips, sharp and almost too much to handle. His eyes watered as they placed him roughly into the back. *At least I won't have this to worry about much longer,* he thought, trying to focus on the bright side.

Oh, Milli, he thought as the ambulance took off, wailing its siren through the streets, *where are you?*

———◆———

'I have to be honest, Karan, this surgery won't be a cakewalk. Neither for me nor for you,' Dr Nathan said, running a hand through his hair. 'I had my doubts about even scheduling this surgery. While your heart condition doesn't make a double hip replacement impossible, it does make it a great deal more difficult. Not to mention the fact that you're so young and have already undergone two heart surgeries,' he sighed. 'But I doubt I'm the first person to tell you that.'

'I sure do hope you'll be the last, though!' Karan quipped. Better to laugh than to cry, especially if something went wrong during his surgery and he didn't wake up. It was a possibility he had juggled since he was a teenager. He had learned quickly to live with the threat of death. If laughing was the last thing you did, you would definitely have the last laugh.

'I have faith in you, Karan,' Dr Nathan said. 'I wouldn't be going ahead with the surgery if I didn't. I certainly wouldn't have flown in all the way from Singapore. I've read the case files, seen the sort of stuff you've overcome. You're a survivor, yeah?'

Karan nodded, as sure of himself as he could be. 'I'm a survivor,' he echoed, 'like that Destiny's Child song.' He hummed it under his breath, smirking at the doctor.

'That's what I like to hear. Your optimism, not that pop song,' Doctor Nathan clarified. 'I want to make sure this puts an end to the pain and misery that the necrosis is putting you through. We're gonna have a one-and-done deal with this surgery. Make sure it's a success, so you get your life back on track.'

The thought of it seemed so alien to Karan, he could only nod, unable to truly internalize the idea of having his life back. Hyperlipidaemia was a chronic condition. He would never truly be free. But he had never been truly captive until he had lost his ability to walk. He was grateful for the surgeon's help.

'You'll be fine, Karan, I promise. You're a lucky guy, huh?'

Karan's mind considered all the good in his life. His family, sitting in the waiting room and their faith that he would pull through. Amit and his steady, strong support. Dr Lox with his supermodel wife and wicked sense of humour, hauling Karan out of his darkest depression. And Milli. Her beautiful smile and soft hands in his.

'Yeah,' he agreed, 'I really am a lucky guy.'

Sixteen

'Bajwa, Milli?' the monotone of a bored doctor's assistant from the doors to the emergency room ward filtered into Milli's ears. She started from the stunned silence she had let herself succumb to, stretching as she rose from the uncomfortable plastic chairs in the emergency room's waiting area. They really ought to buy softer chairs, she thought, working out a crick in her neck as the man told her to follow him. If there was one thing the people in that room needed, it was comfort.

In the ward, an emergency room nurse passed by with a styrofoam cup of black coffee in one hand and a clipboard tucked under her arm. Someone was moaning behind one curtain, an old woman, all alone. Behind another curtain, a couple argued in whispers. A discordant symphony of EKG's, call buttons and flashing codes rose above all the other sounds. An orderly pushed past with a laundry bag of soiled linens. Two nurses at the nurses' station looked over a patient's records together. An Emergency Medical Technician wheeled an empty gurney to a waiting ambulance. It was all Milli could do to follow the assistant as they made their way to her mother's room.

It wasn't a room, really. It was a bed with iatric equipment and gadgets along the rear wall, screened off by curtains with just enough space for one chair. In the bed was her mother, looking small and frail in her hospital gown, surrounded by the medical paraphernalia. She was hooked up to oxygen and an IV. In a bag behind her was some foul, noxious-looking substance that Milli's eyes purposefully avoided. It was like something out of a horror story. Milli's mind couldn't help but drift to Karan's many health problems. How many times in his life had he woken up to a room like this?

'There's good news and there's bad news, Milli,' said the ER doctor. His expression was sombre and his tone, severe. 'The good news is that your mother will survive this overdose. You got her help just in time. If it had been any later, this would be a different conversation.'

Milli let out a sigh of relief. Thank God. Her mother would survive. This nightmare was one step closer to being over. 'Thank you, thank you,' she said, emotion choking her voice.

'We think she might have tried to quit pills, but that the withdrawal was so bad she couldn't take it. Her tolerance lowered and she OD'd. It happens a lot in cases like this. But your mother is very strong. And you did the right thing, calling the ambulance,' the doctor's assurance fell on deaf ears.

'When can I take her home, please?' It was the only thing Milli wanted to know.

'Well, that's where your bad news comes in. Your mother needs rest, Milli. She needs these drugs out of her system so she can begin to heal, but her body is so weak that she might not survive withdrawal unaided.' Milli nodded dumbly, listening to the doctor laying out her worst nightmare for her. 'She'll need to go into rehab, Milli. It can't wait. If she does more pills, she'll die. If she tries to go through withdrawal at home, she'll die. There is no winning without getting medical professionals involved.'

'I can't afford to put her into rehab,' Milli confessed, her voice barely a whisper. 'She has spent every penny we had. She has pawned everything we own. There's nothing left.'

'Can you afford to let her die, Milli?' the doctor asked, looking seriously into Milli's eyes. Milli shook her head, panic rising in her throat. 'Because that's what will happen if she's not sent to rehab.' Milli squeezed her eyes shut. Her mind was swimming with horror.

'Get some rest. I'll come through with a referral for you as soon as possible,' the doctor put a comforting hand on her shoulder.

Milli couldn't look at her mother in that hospital bed or spend another second around that plethora of noisy machines. The wailing of people just as horrified and hurt as she was, around, her was too much to handle. She slunk back to the waiting room in a daze, sinking into a plastic chair before the racking sobs overtook her body.

It was all too much to bear. She had no one. Karan couldn't come to her rescue now. Her brother was long dead. Her mother had put herself in a hospital bed and was heading for the grave herself. There was no one to save Milli from the misery of her own life.

She wasn't sure how long she sat there, sobbing. No one in the room took any notice of her, almost like she was just another grief-stricken ghost haunting the hospital corridors and not a live human being in visible pain. A little girl slept spread across two of the plastic chairs, her exhausted father stroking her hair absently. A man and a woman held each other close as the news played silently in the background. A man who had driven himself to the Emergency Room, muttered to himself as he stared off into nothing. And Milli sobbed, totally alone. She buried her head in her hands. Anything to block out the lights and the noise.

A gentle hand brushed across her shoulder, comforting and careful. At first Milli thought she had imagined the touch, so desperate to be comforted that she couldn't even think clearly about the fact that she was alone and no one was coming to comfort her. But then she felt the hand again and a deep voice close to her ear said, 'Milli?'

Her head snapped up. It was Rahull. He had squeezed his massive frame into the chair next to her and was stroking her shoulder with one massive hand. Milli couldn't even find it in herself to hate him right now. She leaned against him and let him support some of her weight.

'I saw the ambulance pulling away from your house and followed in my car. I thought you might need help,' he said. 'Looks like I was right.'

'Oh, don't you start with me now,' she choked, scrubbing furiously at her tearstained cheeks with her sleeves.

'If you really think I'd start on you when you're in such a bad state, you don't know me at all,' he chided. She could hear the hurt in his voice. She wondered if she really did know him at all, and after all this time. Maybe he was right.

'I'm sorry,' she said. 'I'm just … it's too much right now.'

'Hey, I understand. That's why I'm here,' he rubbed comforting circles into her shoulder. 'Is she going to make it?'

'For now,' Milli couldn't stop the tears from flowing, 'but if I can't get her into rehab, and you know I can't, she won't make it. Either the withdrawal will kill her or the pills will. Remember when she used to make us lemonade, when it was you, me and Karan running around like hooligans in the backyard? What *happened*, Rahull?'

'Life happened, Milli,' he shrugged, and she couldn't even hate him for the pity in his voice. 'Your dad left, your brother died. It was too much for her to handle. Hell, I've always wondered how you handled it as well as you did.'

'I haven't, really,' she replied. 'All the suffering I've been through. It just made me mean.'

'You're not mean, Milli, you're trapped,' he said. 'I've hated seeing you like this all these years, like watching an animal in a cage. The walls kept shrinking around you and I would think, "now she's going to bust through and get out of here once and for all," but you never did. You stayed strong.'

'I didn't know where else to go. Until now, this life was all I knew,' she said, gazing at the sparkling pigment of the floor tiles. 'And now, this life is changing. I don't recognize anything in it anymore.'

'You've still got me,' Rahull said with another shrug, as though he didn't think he was of much value to her at all. But here in the waiting room, when Karan wasn't answering her calls and her mother was suffering in a tiny hospital room, Rahull was the only friend she had in the world. The thought infuriated her. She knew it was irrational, but it wasn't as though he had always been a good friend to her, either. He could be selfish and cruel.

'I don't want you,' she snapped. She couldn't regret her tone, even though she wanted to apologize for it.

'I can tell,' he told her, pointing to her hand, 'you're not wearing my ring.'

Milli released a laugh that felt strange in her throat, a little too hysterical. 'No,' she gasped, 'I'm not. But Mama is,' she laughed again, unable to help herself. The weird image of her mother's hand in the ambulance seemed absurd to her now, with the lack of sleep and abundance of horror coursing through her body like a drug. 'My mother is wearing your ring.'

'Milli, what in the world are you saying?' Rahull asked, alarmed. The couple in the chair across from them shot Milli a dirty look as her laughter rang out across the silent waiting room. Milli gasped, still laughing, and tried to catch her breath.

'I don't know what she was doing with it. Probably she was gonna pawn it first chance she got, like she did her own wedding ring. Maybe she wanted to look at something pretty for a change. I don't know,' and suddenly Milli's laughter transformed into a sob. Rahull held her through it, his huge arms holding her tight, protected. 'She's always telling me I should marry you. Maybe— maybe, she was secretly in love with you all along. Maybe—'

'Maybe we should pawn it,' he muttered above her. At first, Milli thought she had misheard him.

'What did you say?' she asked, looking up at him through her tears. He met her gaze steadily.

'I said, "maybe we should pawn it."' he repeated. 'What? Don't give me that look. You clearly don't want to marry me. And even if you did, I wouldn't marry you right now, not with you this miserable. You're not fit to be getting married right now. You're in too much trouble to think clearly. You need help, not a husband.'

'I—I don't understand,' Milli stuttered.

'Listen, do you want to marry me?' Rahull asked, seriously.

'No,' she replied immediately. He nodded, as though he had known the answer all along.

'And I don't want to be in a one-sided marriage. I don't want to be the person who ties you down forever. And frankly, I'm starting to think I don't want to be tied to you, either.'

'Huh!' Milli exclaimed, mock-offended. Her smile was showing in spite of herself. It seemed Rahull had finally understood that there was no point forcing a relationship on Milli as she would never give in to something she doesn't really want.

'Not that you aren't the prettiest girl in Chandigarh, because we all know you are. But I want to set my sights farther than Chandigarh. And I want to find somebody who loves me. I couldn't do that, tied down to you. So, I've been thinking about it and I retract my proposal. Ms Milli Bajwa, will you do me the honour of never, ever becoming my wife?' he teased.

And maybe it was that he still knew how to make her smile, or that something in his eyes reminded her of the children they had once been together, but in that moment, Milli finally stopped hating Rahull. Instead, she envisioned a future where they might one day be friends.

'Mr Rahull Suri,' she responded with just as much mock solemnity, 'the honour of never marrying you is all mine.' He ruffled her hair, laughing as he tucked her back into his side.

'Well, that settles that,' he told her, 'but it doesn't settle anything else in your life.'

'Don't I know it?' Milli sighed. Her tears had dried for now but the feeling of terror in her gut still remained. She was in way over her head.

'What did the doctor say about your mother?'

'Overdose. I mean, the vomit, the pills, the blue lips and limp body,' Milli's hand started to tremble and she clenched her fist. 'The doctors are saying she either needs rehab or she'll die. She won't be able to kick the habit on her own.'

'So we'll get her into rehab,' Rahull assured her.

'With what damn money?' Milli hissed. 'You don't understand. She took everything. I owe on the house, she re-mortgaged that, she's stolen every paisa she could find in my purse, my oatmeal jar, everything is gone, Rahull. Insurance won't cover what it would cost to put her in one of these fancy places. We're in more trouble than we've ever been in, even since my brother's death,' she declared finally. 'I'm the only one who can solve it for us but I don't even know where to begin.'

'Well, then, we'll just have to sit down, think it over, and figure it out,' he decided. 'I've never met a problem without a solution.'

'And the worst part of all of this,' Milli blurted, unable to stop talking now that she had finally confessed, 'is that I met a man.

A beautiful, sensitive, clever man who could finally take me away from this place. But I can't leave with him. Not if it means my mother is going to die,' tears streamed down her face again as though they had never stopped. 'But I suppose you'll probably hate me, now that I've told you that.'

'I don't hate you, Milli,' Rahull told her. 'I already knew. Last time I saw you, you had this look in your eyes. Like you were already gone. I hated to see it but I could never hate you,' he rubbed her shoulder.

'You're a good man, Rahull,' Milli said. She meant it, too. She never thought she would.

'And don't you forget it,' he smiled. 'Listen, I think I can help you, with the house if nothing else. But that means one less thing in your life to worry about. Money to pay the mortgage and save your mother. I don't know if you're going to like it, though.'

'Even if I don't like it,' she replied, 'I can't hate it as much as I hate this situation. I'm backed into a corner, Rahull. And if it doesn't involve marrying you, I suppose I'm down to try anything that you think might help. What's the plan?'

———◆———

Dawn was breaking over the horizon, barely visible through the dim windows of the hospital cafeteria. Milli had been told by the on-call nurse that her mother's condition was serious but stable. The only thing left to do was wait for her body to expel the rest of the poison she had put into it, but that would take time. Milli and Rahull spent most of the night plotting their way out of misery and had settled upon something that might work for both of them. As much as the plan shocked Milli, it would do the job of freeing her, saving her mother, and preserving their family home.

She was going to sell the house to Rahull.

She had to think of her family home as a fixer-upper property that backed up into Rahull's farm, so that the Suri's could expand their legacy and Rahull could physically build a place of his own from the ruins of the Bajwa house. He would take her mother on as a tenant once she got out of rehab and let her stay, rent-free, where he could keep an eye on her. Milli would be homeless, but she would be happy. She would be free.

And she was beginning to think that she had found a home anyway. She couldn't wait to come home and tell Karan what she had found. All she could think about was curling up in his arms. How proud he would be of her, to know that she had worked out the problem most bothering her, and that now they would be free to live their lives together! Milli was ready for that day to begin.

Milli and Rahull were in line for a cup of coffee. Rahull hadn't even put up a token resistance at the thought of letting her pay for his cup. Perhaps he was still trying to comfort her but Milli felt that he was actually trying to be her friend. It could work. All of this could work.

As she turned to find a table, she came face to face with a familiar man.

'Amit?' she said. He looked as surprised to see her as she was to see him.

'Well, there you are,' he said, staring in shock. 'Here to see Karan?'

'Karan's here? In the hospital?' Any relief Milli felt immediately abated. Stress tightened in her chest. Her mouth felt dry. 'What happened?'

'His hip replacement,' Amit said, 'the doctor moved his surgery up a day. He's in surgery now. You won't be able to see him so long as they're operating, but his parents are in the family waiting room. You can meet them there if you'd like."

'Yes, can I see them please?' she asked, before remembering where she was and who she was currently waiting to see. She turned to Rahull, unsure of what to tell him.

Nonetheless, it seemed he understood. 'Go,' he nodded, lifting his cup of coffee in salute. 'I'll stay with your mother. Go on.'

Amit let her know where they would be when she was ready to find them. Milli didn't hesitate. Her coffee in hand, she ran.

SEVENTEEN

If Milli hadn't loved Karan before meeting the rest of his family, she surely loved him now. Surrounded by three people just as dark and severe-looking as Karan was, but with the same quirking smile and light-hearted ability to quip in the face of tragedy, she felt completely at home. There was nothing more reassuring to Milli than knowing that the man she loved had a family who loved him, in stark contrast to her dysfunctional family. They were peaceful, even in the face of such adversity. They had opened their arms to Milli as soon as Amit brought her to them, introducing her mainly as Karan's 'good friend' and saying little else about her.

They hadn't asked unnecessary questions or wondered too hard about just what a woman with tired eyes and someone else's vomit staining the sleeve of her shirt was doing waiting for their son to recover from a surgery she didn't even known he was having. It didn't seem to faze them, although Milli could make an educated guess that they were the kind of people that few things fazed. Karan's father was a powerful and imposing man, with broader shoulders than Karan and with straight hair.

Karan's curls and easy posture came from his mother, a woman with few lines on her face and shrewd, assessing eyes that seemed to know exactly who Milli was. The easy smile on her face seemed to imply that she approved of Milli, even though the girl wasn't anything close to what she was used to seeing from Karan's array of vapid girlfriends.

Milli wasn't sure how much his family knew about Karan's failures in love and friendship with women who only wanted him for his money. Somehow, despite the relative rags she was dressed in in comparison to Karan's wealthy family, they seemed to understand that Milli's poverty was an easy and comfortable thing for her, and that she was not looking for a way out of it with Karan's money. Karan's mother's eyes conveyed an understanding Milli had only ever seen in Karan's own coffee-coloured eyes. She wondered where Karan's mother had come from and if it might have been the same hills where Milli was raised.

Most obviously approving and loving of all of Karan's family was his younger sister, Mallvika, who told Milli early on that she had avoided the family business and much of her responsibility in favour of pursuing a degree in theatre history. Her father frowned in mock-disapproval, but it was clear from the smile on his face that he didn't hold a grudge against his daughter for following her passions. He seemed genuinely please she had found it. Mallvika was more free than any person Milli had seen before, easy with her laugh and generous with her smile. She had been the one to deal Milli into the Go-Fish game that she swore was a family hospital tradition.

Milli enjoyed the game but couldn't help but feel a little sad that she was joining a family who had 'hospital traditions'. Still, it didn't seem to bother any of the family to her untrained eye, at least at first. Indeed, it seemed until she had settled into the game truly, that they were entirely unconcerned about Karan's progress in the operating room. But then she caught the perpetual clearing of Karan's father's throat, the way his mother glanced from time to time at an elegant silver wrist-watch, the way that Mallvika's over-bright smile and bold laugh made her parents wince as though it were a couple of decibels higher than its usual pitch. *They're terrified*, Milli thought. *Just like me.*

But they were past masters at combatting their own terror, able to fight off the sense of dread and worry that a person felt when their loved one was sick with a heady blend of optimism and humour that was infectious in the small, usually sad rooms where families waited, hoping for good news from the doctors and nurses on the other side. They lightened the space they were in, because they were so used to darkness.

The realization made Milli's soul feel less heavy. No longer was she fretting about her mother being intubated and prodded by nurses trying to resurrect her battered body into life and health. No longer was she imagining a scalpel cutting away Karan's dead flesh and accidentally slipping, nicking an artery they couldn't sew shut before the anticoagulants in his blood forced the life from his body. Instead, she was worrying that Amit might not have any eights and that she would fall behind Mallvika into third place with no hope of beating Karan's father, who may or may not be cheating in order to beat them all at Go-Fish. She let out a laugh, surprised to discover that she truly meant it. No one had even said anything that funny. But their optimism was like lifeblood in her veins and Milli felt alive.

Mallvika sent a smile her way, the same one that had appeared on Karan's face before. Questioning, and overjoyed. 'Are you winning?' she asked, 'it doesn't look like it to me.'

'Me neither,' Milli agreed, 'but in spite of myself, I just can't seem to shake the feeling that I'm doing really well.'

'That's how you've got to do it,' Karan's mother agreed. Her voice was quieter than her husband's booming baritone or her daughter's laughter, and it contained a note of strength that was pure, cold steel. Milli hoped that one day the trials she had been through would give her that same solid core. 'In spite of what it might look like, you've got to think that you're winning. It's the only way to never end up defeated.'

'No matter what happens,' it was Amit who covered her hand with his.

'I'm out,' Karan's father declared. They all turned to look at him, mouths agape. 'What?' he asked. The whole family launched into an argument they didn't mean, laughing as Karan's father presented more and more ridiculous claims as to just how much they all owed him at the end of the reckoning. It sounded like a home to Milli. Something she hadn't heard in a long time.

———•———

Karan's first conscious thought when his eyes opened in the post-anaesthesia care unit was that the PACU reeked. A sweet and sour smell of antiseptic and vomit greeted him. The world around him swam with green and white light, sterile and fluorescent in his vision. Time was an illusion, rushing past so hours felt like seconds, then freezing in place so a four-second span felt like a day. He let his eyes drift shut. One moment he was aware of the IV in his arm, the next moment of his immobility. He had only a second to alert the PACU nurse before he vomited once more. *Oh, that's what that smell is,* he thought dizzily, before drifting back into darkness.

He had no dreams in his unnatural sleep. The world moved around him like shadows flickering in his peripheral vision. It made no difference whether his eyes were open or closed at first. The nurse administered more medication to him and the press of nausea in his gut abated. There was no weight in his chest, no sensation in his body. Just a fuzzy, cool feeling. His breath moved in and out of his body. His body had changed. But one thing remained the same. The beating of his heart, unsteady, but his own, declared what it always had: *I'm alive. I'm alive. I'm alive.*

Hello, body. Hello, blood. Hello, new hips and old heart and new pain. Karan cherished it all. The rise and fall of his chest was proof enough that the pain was worth it. He had survived.

———•———

Milli examined a teddy bear in the gift shop with distaste. Its neon purple fur was garish and its 'get well soon!' placard seemed trite given the situation at hand. It would feel like a slap in the face to her mother if Milli left it with her and given Karan's operation, the sentiment seemed inadequate to say the least. Mallvika, at the next counter, was peering at a snow globe with a pink baby carriage in it. Picking it up, she shook it and stared into the floating flecks of glitter suspended in baby oil as though she would be able to discern the future in its patterns.

'He might like this,' she said. At Milli's expression, she gave a shrug. 'What? I know it's not appropriate for the situation at hand, but they don't make cards for this kind of stuff – "Sorry, bad stuff keeps happening to you, I don't get it either but I love you and will be there for this surgery and the next one" doesn't exactly scream 'Hallmark', now does it?'

'I suppose you're right,' Milli said, 'and it might make him laugh.' *When all this is over and he can laugh about anything,* she thought, but did not dare voice it in front of Karan's sister. This had been Mallvika's reality for far longer than it had been Milli's. Surely, she wouldn't appreciate Milli reminding her of her brother's grim reality any more than the hospital walls already did.

'Oh, he'll laugh again sooner than you think,' Mallvika reassured her, examining garden rocks that read *faith, hope* and *love* in curling font across their fronts. 'There are two things consistent about Karan's life: his rotten luck and his sunny disposition about the whole thing,' she smiled to herself, as though remembering some joke for which Milli had not been present, 'although something tells me his luck has changed a little.'

'How do you mean?' Milli asked, running a finger absently across a photoframe's edge.

'You know exactly what I mean,' Mallvika smiled, weighing the rocks in her hand. 'He's got you to take care of him now. That's more luck than he's ever had, right there.'

Milli wasn't sure what to say to that. She felt like the lucky one just to know someone like Karan. To get to hold him. To call him her own. But before she could reply, Mallvika continued, 'I'm thinking about getting him these rocks. If he's immobile for a little while, he'll need some sort of projectile to chuck at the swans in case they get testy and try to start an uprising.'

'Do the swans get testy often?' Milli asked, coming over to study the rocks. 'I think we could find him a better defence system than three rocks. How would he retrieve them while his legs are recovering from the surgery?'

'Excellent point,' Mallvika told her, setting the rocks back down on the shelf with a sigh. 'Maybe I'll get some of these stuffed animals. Make a scarecrow. Scare-swan,' she let out a huge yawn, stretching. 'But later. All this can be done later. Come on, let's go back to the family lounge and stare blankly at whatever Adam Sandler movie they've got close-captioned on the TV until we fall asleep. Karan should be out of surgery soon if he's not already.'

Milli nodded. She had been following Mallvika and chatting most of the night since the family had finished their third consecutive game of Go Fish and retired to the fold-out couches for the evening. Mallvika was as restless as Milli was. They had raided the cafeteria, sipped cups of nasty black coffee at the counter while talking about Karan's childhood and Milli's dreams into the wee hours of the morning.

Then they had run outside for some fresh air and ended up finding the opposite. Three ER nurses, speaking up clouds of cigarette smoke that clung to the girls' clothes, told them about their evening. One of them had Milli's mother on her rotation and assured Milli that her mother was already looking better. 'Trust me, in three weeks, she'll be thriving,' the nurse told Milli. 'Ridgeview does wonders with their rehab work. I've got a girlfriend who works over there. She loves it.'

Mallvika could sense Milli's discomfort with the conversation, which was how they had ended up in the gift shop. 'Come on,' she said, tugging Milli towards the hospital doors, 'let's go buy our family a bunch of weird useless stuff they'll end up forgetting about and leaving in the waiting room.'

Our family, Milli thought. She had never been accepted by anyone like this, much less so quickly. She couldn't help but smile.

Now they were heading back into the family lounge at Mallvika's urging with all the speed and determination of someone who knew well how to distract themselves from the tragedy of having a loved one hospitalized. Milli was grateful for Mallvika's friendship. It was obvious that she was Karan's sister. Even if they didn't have the same aquiline nose and dark, curling hair, they shared the same abundant kindness and unruffled attitude despite trouble and tragedy. That happiness in their lives, evident even through their pain, couldn't be faked.

Of course, now that Milli had met Karan's parents, it was easy to see where that happiness that ran so profusely through both him and his sister had originated. His mother was warm, sweet and considerate in the way she handled her family; strong as iron in the face of tragedy. She was beautiful, possessing a grace that Milli had only envisioned in the stoic queens of yore. And her husband was a king. Although he carried the weight of the empire he had built on his shoulders, he smiled easily. It was easy to see how Karan fitted into his family. He was a young prince among royalty.

Milli couldn't help but feel like a fish out of water. It hadn't helped that when she had met Karan's parents, Amit had stepped in, introducing her as 'Karan's friend'. But what were they, if not friends? She loved him, sure, but they hadn't had that much time to talk about what they were to each other and what they wanted before fate had intervened, separating them. They had mentioned the term 'boyfriend' once, and even then, it was still so new that Milli couldn't be sure he meant it. She knew she loved him. She knew he loved her. But until they decided to be anything else, 'friends' seemed the least complicated relationship.

In any case, Karan's mother had accepted Milli's handshake with such grace that Milli couldn't help but think they *knew* somehow what their son meant to her. Milli could feel it warm like a sunbeam in her gentle smile. Despite the cool introduction she had received, her welcome was a warm one.

Perhaps Karan's condition meant he had few people in his life anyway, friends or otherwise. Certainly, from what he had told Milli, he had only a handful of people who didn't have a vested interest in spending his money. So, to see Milli in her work slacks and collared shirt, her frizzy hair and crooked teeth, it must have put them at ease. Clearly, she had never known money and hadn't gotten a taste for it. She wasn't the sort of woman to sink her teeth into Karan.

When Milli and Mallvika arrived back at the family lounge, Karan's parents were wide awake, and in deep conversation with the surgeon. 'Ah, Mallvika,' Karan's mother summoned her daughter to her side. Milli hovered awkwardly for only a moment before Mallvika made a quick gesture with her fingers, indicating that it was okay to approach.

'Milli, this is Dr Suresh Nathan,' Mallvika introduced smoothly as though there had been no moment of awkwardness between Milli and Karan's parents in the slightest. 'The man is a genius, a well-known doctor from Singapore who is at the forefront of operations like Karan's. He flew in just for our boy.'

'Wouldn't have missed it for the world,' the doctor replied cheerily. 'Your Karan is a nightmare patient, between the heart condition and the scars he's sustained from surgeries. But I wouldn't have missed a challenge like this one for the world. His story touched me. Performing this surgery was a very different experience in my professional experience so far.'

'We're happy that you could come,' Karan's father replied.

'Your son is a real fighter. And I come with good news,' Dr Nathan assured them. 'Karan's surgery was an astounding success, especially given all the barriers he had to overcome. The nurses are a little disappointed that they don't get to paint his nails, but they're the only ones who are even the slightest bit upset. I'm close to doing cartwheels.'

Milli's heart gave a leap of joy at the doctor's words. She could barely hear what was said next. The look she exchanged with Mallvika suggested that Mallvika's heart shared the same joy. 'Thank God,' Karan's mother whispered, 'thank God.'

'He's out of the PACU and in the post-surgery recovery room. He'll be able to see visitors now for a few moments. Preferably one at a time; try not to tire him out. Come with me, I'll lead you to him.' They made their way down the sterile hallway to where Karan lay.

Milli's stomach twisted with nerves.

'He's never had a surgery quite like this one but his recovery won't be an easy one,' the surgeon explained. 'I can't promise you how conscious he'll be, but what I can tell you is that he's in a great deal of pain, so be gentle. Hushed voices.' They stood in the corridor outside room 571 where nurses moved quietly through the halls on their rounds, consulting charts and pushing trays full of jello and pudding. 'He can't be moved for three days after the surgery. After eight days, he can rest at home. And in three weeks, therapy can begin. He can have his family during visiting hours, but I'm afraid only one of you will be allowed to stay in the room at night.'

Mallvika and her parents exchanged a look. 'We'll talk about it after we see him,' Karan's mother said decidedly.

'He's right through here,' Dr Nathan gestured, 'and may even be conscious, although I'm not sure how long he'll stay that way,' and with that, they entered the room.

Any fears that Milli had that she might be horrified on seeing him were abated when his eyes met hers. He looked exhausted, yes, worse than she had ever seen him. But the warmth in his eyes, the weak smile he tried to muster at the sight of her, that was all Karan. Milli would do anything for that smile. His magnetic eyes drew her closer, before she even realized what was happening.

'Milli,' he breathed. He was all she could see. She forgot about the hospital room around them and his family standing behind her.

'I'm here,' she said breathlessly.

'Well, that settles who will be sleeping here tonight,' Mallvika snorted. Her mother raised an eyebrow, but both she and Karan's father were smiling.

'Mom, Dad, Mallvika,' Karan mustered up enough energy to voice their names. "I'm so glad to see you."

Karan's mother hurried to his bedside. She did not touch him, but the force of her presence alone, maternal and comforting, seemed to strengthen him. He gave her a smile, bringing her hand to his lips to kiss it. 'You won't break me,' he said. One by one his family fell in, kissing him soundly, joy evident on their faces. Milli remained by the door, aware she was intruding on a private family moment.

Then Karan glimpsed Milli once more. He opened his mouth but no sound came out. His eyes closed as he gathered his strength. When he opened them again, everyone in the room, Milli included, were looking at him expectantly.

'Mom, Dad, this is my girlfriend, Milli,' he said. 'She's beautiful and I love her.'

Milli's eyes widened as she realized just what he had said. She blushed furiously but the smile that erupted on her face couldn't be contained. He loved her and she loved him, too. And now everyone knew.

'I love you, too, Karan,' she said

Mallvika laughed. Karan's mother covered her smile with her hand, squeezing her husband's hand with the other. 'Well,' she said, 'we're glad to meet her, Karan. We enjoyed the time we spent with her in the waiting room. You're a lucky man.'

'And she's a lucky girl to have you,' Karan's father reminded him. He gave Milli a warm wink.

'I am, Sir,' she told him. She sank into the chair across from his bed and held his hand in hers. His grip was weak, but he squeezed back nonetheless.

'Karan,' his mother spoke gently as she observed the tired lines of his face, 'we're going back to the hotel room to rest. We'll be back first thing in the morning. If you like, I'll let Amit know that he can stay home and rest as well. I think Milli has you covered.'

'Yes, let him know,' Karan agreed, his eyes fluttering shut, 'she's got me.'

'I do,' Milli whispered as his family left the room.

He didn't answer her for he was sound asleep once more. Milli gave a happy sigh as she flipped the lights down low. Just until the nurses came through again, she would rest her eyes. Karan would need her strength in the morning. She located the fold-out mattress on his other side and stacked two hypoallergenic pillows under her neck. She turned on her side so she could watch Karan's chest rising and falling, illuminated by the dim light from the monitors.

———•———

The next morning, Milli left Karan sleeping, confident that a note and a word with the nurse making rounds would be enough to put him at ease. She made her way down to the ICU, asking for her mother. The nurse smiled.

'Bajwa? Good news. Your mother's moved up to the psych floor now that she's stable. She needs rest and some more observation until we determine she's of no risk to herself. She pulled through and we'll be sending her home soon.' Milli bit her lip to keep from crying. Whether out of relief or fear, she wasn't sure. When the good news was that your mother was in the psych ward, it was a mixed blessing for sure. Still, she kept reminding herself that her mother had survived. Anything else that happened afterward would be a step on her path to healing.

The next time Milli saw her mother, she was sitting up, seemingly conscious, but staring at nothing. Her eyes were glued to a spot below the television and did not flicker to glance at Milli when she entered the room. Her lips were pursed in a thin line.

'Mama?' She hated how her voice quavered, suddenly weak after so much time spent trying to be strong. Now that she was past the relief of knowing her mother would survive, now that she had Karan safely on the other side of his surgery, there was nothing left for which she needed to be strong. Now it was only her, her mother and the ocean of pain between them that Milli didn't know how to cross.

Her mother didn't answer. Milli wasn't sure whether this was because she was just too sick to respond or if she was ashamed of the trouble she had caused her daughter. Ambulances weren't cheap. Hospital bills weren't cheap. A woman who had spent her whole life counting pennies must have calculated the cost of the suffering she had wrought.

Her mother sighed, finally, a noise that Milli relished because it meant her mother was still breathing. 'Milli,' came her answer. It was a husky breath, so quiet that it was barely audible over the flickering of the TV. 'I've been…'

She trailed off, as if just the effort in voicing her thoughts exhausted her. She wanted Milli to speak for her, to opiate her guilt with assurances of eternal love and devotion but Milli couldn't afford that sort of sympathy.

'You've been a fool, is what you've been,' Milli snapped, suddenly furious. 'You've been ruinous. You've nearly destroyed everything we had and we never had much to begin with. Don't you see that?'

She had to swallow the fury she felt rising like bile in her throat, choking her with every word that came out. The abject poverty they had lived in, where everything from empty jars to broken paper clips were repurposed to some use, where they had learned to make up for the things they lacked by holding all things they had sacred, had permeated the very essence of Milli's being. She had learned to value and love her family from her mother, because it was the most precious thing they had. And now her mother had thrown it all into jeopardy. For what? A handful of pills she had swallowed too quickly? A momentary escape she hoped would last the rest of her life?

'It was cowardly, Mama. Not just the overdose. The first pill you ever swallowed was a coward's move. I've been struggling to fill the gap Karan left and found myself trying to fill the gap you left, too. You're not living with me anymore. You're just haunting me.'

'You should have let me die,' her mother whispered. Milli could feel her face turning red.

'Should I have? Is that what you wanted, Mama? To leave me alone without a friend in this world, to watch me from a cloud of painkillers in heaven as I struggled and failed? Because if you did then there's no love left in you for anything but that pill bottle.'

'Tried … to give you Rahull,' her mother trailed off, leaning back against the pillow. At once, Milli understood both her mother's pushiness and Rahull's. They had each been trying to save her, in their own way. But Milli was resourceful. She was trying to save herself.

'I didn't want Rahull,' she said, 'and you knew that. He knew it too.'

'I know that. It's not about want. It's about need. You needed things and I couldn't—'

'I'm tired of living a life of need!' Milli dropped her hands to her sides, trying to curb her inclination to shape them into fists. 'I should be allowed to want things and to have at least some of the things I want. I want to drink sun tea and read romance novels in the shade in peace. I want to take an airplane to Franc or to at least be allowed to take the time to daydream about it without worrying that my time might be better spent fixing something you broke. I want a break from my life, from needing you and not having you. And I want a mother who acts like she's my mother again!' The tears were streaming down Milli's face.

Her mother's eyes fluttered shut against the onslaught of Milli's words, sheer exhaustion seeping into her body at trying to hold upright even her meagre weight. But Milli wasn't willing to let her off the hook that easily. She didn't want her mother to tune out the hurt she had caused, the way she tried to do with the pills and the booze. She felt as though she had been letting her mother off the hook all her life. Her mother might be broken and useless as a mother but Milli would find another use for her, and love and cherish her just the same. It didn't make sense to let her go.

'Wake up, Mama, because I'm not finished. I met a man,' her mother's eyes opened at that. She stared at Milli, lips pursed, waiting for her to continue. 'He's a good man. Kind and careful. He bears the weight of my body when I'm so tired that I can't sleep, and holds the weight of my hurt even when he can barely stand his own. He's not only what I need, he's what I want, as well. Life with him won't be easy. But it will be good. I don't expect a life of ease. I've never had one before. But I've never had a good life, either, and I'm so, so ready for it.'

The look on her mother's face was one she didn't recognize: it was a peculiar expression, as though she was looking at Milli and seeing a stranger. It occurred to Milli that maybe her mother had never felt that way about a man or anyone. Her mother had never had more than scraps of love, a taste that hadn't lingered long on her tongue before it was replaced by the familiar bitterness of a life lived in struggle. There was envy in her expression, sure, but more than that there was relief. Peace. It was an alien expression coming from her mother. But Milli thought it made her look younger, somehow.

'I'm going to help you through rehab. I'm selling the house to Rahull and from that money, I'm going to pay off the mess you've made of the house and save us. He'll lease it to me while you're getting back on your feet, until you're out of rehab. And when you're gone—' the word stuck in her throat. A wave of shock rushed over her as she realized, like waking up from a dream, that only hours ago she hadn't known whether her mother would survive or not. 'Well, he'll move somebody else in there. And it won't hold anything of ours but the memories. Good riddance to those.'

She expected her mother to complain, to raise a fuss about selling her childhood home. But her mother seemed relieved to have the weight of that house off her shoulders. Milli wondered how many ghosts it held for her mother. Maybe more than Milli had ever felt. Maybe more than she would ever know.

'Milli,' her mother's voice quavered – perhaps she was afraid, too – 'the kind of help I'm going to need. Rehab. We can't afford—' she swallowed, then tried again. 'There's nothing leftthat we can use, to help me get better,' and she was too weak to heal on her own at this point. Milli could read the thoughts her mother didn't dare voice: *maybe you should have let me go.*

'Don't worry, Mama,' she said. 'I've got some money saved. And Karan—' her mother's eyes opened wide and it occurred to Milli that her mother wasn't the only one of the two of them to have kept a secret. 'Not my brother, Karan, but Karan, my…my love. He said he'd help us. That if I needed my Mama, he'd fight to make sure I had you. Whatever it takes.'

Her mother's eyes watered with an emotion that might have been hope if she was still capable of feeling such a thing. 'Oh, Milli,' she breathed. Milli moved to her mother's bedside, gripping her mother's hand in hers. It was so frail and small. She remembered when she was a little girl her mother's presence seemed to tower over her, a comforting shadow cast over everything she did. Now, she was grown. She could protect her mother from the pain of this world, just like her mother had tried to do for her.

'I'm so glad you found love,' her mother whispered as she drifted back to sleep. Milli said nothing, only squeezing her mother's hand tighter in response.

Eighteen

Milli flinched as the front door slammed shut harder than she had intended for it to. She still wasn't entirely used to the size and weight of the ornate door to Karan's mansion. It certainly wasn't the swinging screen door on her old front porch. But inside Karan's cold mansion was a treasure she valued more than anything else in this world.

'Take care, if you please, Milli!' Amit bellowed from somewhere inside the house. 'That door is vintage and quite irreplaceable, especially in terms of the sentiments attached to it.'

'I'm sorry, Amit,' she called back, peering around the corner, where he was dusting the piano room. She gave him a smile she knew he'd always forgive and was rewarded by an answering grin, 'I'm a little graceless today.'

'If you weren't in such a rush, you might find yourself steadier on your feet,' he clucked his tongue, brushing past her as he headed for the kitchen, Karan's empty water bottle in hand.

'If there weren't so many things I needed to rush around for, you might be right,' she agreed, tossing her hair over her shoulder as she pulled the sunglasses off her head and tucked them into their case. She hung her purse on a peg in the entrance hall. 'Is the physiotherapist in yet?'

'I just let her van into the driveway,' Amit said. 'She seemed lovely on the phone.'

'Didn't she just?' Milli drawled, smiling wider as she paused her ascent up the staircase. 'She's so sweet, perhaps he won't even complain about the torture she's putting him through.'

'I don't think anyone's sweet enough to make him forget to complain. Only person he doesn't seem annoyed with these days is you,' Amit laughed.

'I have my ways,' she chuckled, bounding up the stairs.

'Hope your mother was well,' Amit called after her. 'Did you tell her we all say hello and wish her the best?' But Milli was already upstairs. She remembered the first time she had come to this house, almost a month ago now, how confusing it had been. Now she felt as though she could find her way through its halls even in her sleep. Of course, the only place she ever needed to be was Karan's room, where the man himself lay on the bed, reading one of his volumes of poetry.

Music blared from his speakers as he listened, a rousing classical number that Milli thought she recognised from her days in elementary school music classes and that she liked well enough. 'Mozart today, Karan?' she asked, leaning in to give him a kiss.

'Beethoven, actually,' he said with a smile, wincing as he leaned up. 'How is your mother?'

'Anything short of puking on my shoes the way she did last time is a marked improvement, I suppose,' she shrugged. 'Beethoven. Isn't that the St Bernard in that movie?' she asked, all mock innocence, smiling widely as he swiped lazily at her shoulder, a gesture that was closer to a caress than anything else.

'Careful before I leap up out of this bed and chase you,' he teased, his characteristic grin bright on his face. It held Milli captive. She darted carefully out of his way but couldn't keep her eyes off his face.

'And I wish you would, darling, but your PT is in the driveway and imagine how upset she'd be if she caught you running down the hallway.' Milli began to straighten the room around her. There wasn't much of a mess but she wanted it perfect before anyone came in. Their love nest wasn't for anyone else's eyes. 'Do you need to go to the bathroom before she gets here?' she asked. Karan grimaced.

'I'm already in enough pain without moving any more than the physiotherapist will make me,' he responded, 'I'll wait.'

'You'll just hurt worse after she's done with you,' Milli warned.

'After a certain point, it's all relative,' he retorted. 'We've got pain in abundance around here. What's a little more?'

'I suppose that's the spirit,' she said, returning Karan's books to the stack on the shelf.

'Hey,' he groaned, reaching for the book she had lifted from his bedside table, 'I was reading that.'

'And I'll keep reading it to you tonight after dinner. But we want the PT to think that this is a bedroom, not a barn, so I'm cleaning up this mess before she opens the door.'

'I don't know how these things get so messy. I promise I'm not running around after you leave making a mess just for the fun of it,' he teased, 'Even though I wish I could.'

He sighed and her heart broke a little. She pressed a kiss to Karan's cheek. He returned it by kissing her on the lips. She smiled into his touch, so happy to have him by her side that the world around them seemed immaterial for a moment. She forgot where she was and lost herself in Karan's kiss.

There was a knock at the door and they pulled apart. Milli tucked an errant strand of hair behind her ear as she went to answer the door.

The PT nurse had dark hair pulled back into a sleek ponytail and an unwavering, gentle smile that would put even the most irritable man at ease. Through these hard times when Karan was suffering so much, it was good to know that his doctors and therapist were gentle, careful people who would smile for him when his own smile wavered.

It put Milli at ease, too. She was in a whole new world with Karan. Her mother was in rehab, slowly but surely getting better. Rahull had installed a new washbasin in the bathroom and was meeting with Milli this weekend to straighten out the crooked fence that she had set up herself. Plants were flourishing in the garden and her life with Karan was coming into full bloom.

It hurt to watch him hurt but when he accomplished a little more Milli's heart felt as though it might soar out of her chest. The way he would look up at her and smile with that infectious grin that said, 'told you I could do this,' Milli would smile right back because she loved him so and she had never doubted him. Even when he was sweaty, muscles exhausted, too tired to do more than lift his head, she would hold hers high with the pride she felt in him.

'If I didn't have you,' he told her one night, long after they had turned the lights out and her head was pillowed on his chest, 'I don't think I'd have the strength to take another step.'

His confession lingered for a long moment in the darkness between them. It hurt to hear just how close he had been to losing that spark of strength in him before she met him. But she knew just what to say to help him heal. To help that spark catch flame. 'Then I'll be here until you can run. I'll stay here until you can fly through the air.'

'With you, the wind beneath my wings?' he teased, but she could see the smile on his face even in the darkness.

'With me,' she agreed, pulling him in close and planting a kiss on his temple. 'Any time you need that boost of strength, look to me. I'd give you all of mine if I could. Watching you succeed has been the most incredible gift you've ever given me. I'm so grateful every time I see you take that extra step, even when I can see the pain you're in and your muscles straining with the effort.' Words spilled from her now, and while she couldn't see his expression, she could feel his body tense as he listened to her. Every muscle alert in the darkness. Careful, cautious, taking it all in. He felt like she did: amazed that they had found each other, stunned to know that there was another person on the planet who had the same soul. 'To know you're trying and to see you doing better than what the physiotherapist even thought possible when we started. To know that I'm the one blessed enough to wipe the sweat from your brow and offer you my shoulder to rest on at the end of it. I've never loved anyone so much in my life.'

There was silence between them for a moment filled only by the distant sound of tree frogs in the dark and grass swishing in the night breeze. When Karan spoke after a long pause, heavy with thought, his voice was serious and deliberate.

'The very day that I can walk again,' he told her, 'I am walking to the jewellery counter and buying you the largest diamond that will fit on your finger. And then I'll walk down the aisle and I will marry you, Milli Bajwa, in the sight of God and everyone.'

The birds fluttering in her chest took flight. When she kissed him, her body sang like a symphony. His breath against her cheek felt like heaven. His lips against hers, the faint scrape of stubble across her face, everything was real and wonderful. Her body lit up like she had been plugged into an electric socket as Karan deepened the kiss. She was flying without wings, like he had said in his poem once. She never wanted their journey together to end. Knowing that this was just the start of the golden days of their lives made her feel alive. Everything before Karan was a bad dream. This waking life was better than anything she could imagine behind her closed eyelids.

'I'd marry you in a wheelchair just as easily as I'd marry you on two feet,' she told him breathlessly when she pulled away, her hands still clinging to his skin. She was intoxicated with his words and the feeling of his body so close to hers. 'But I'm willing to wait as long as you want to wait.' With that he kissed her again, his lips searing and searching against hers. What he found in Milli's kiss must have pleased him. She could feel his warm smile widening against her lips.

'But I have a feeling that, either way, we won't have to wait that long,' she told him, a teasing whisper in his ear, before losing herself again in his kiss. When she pulled away again, hours later, the first rays of morning light were spilling through the cracks in the blind. The sun was rising on their new life together and everything existed for Milli in this perfect moment of tranquillity.

EPILOGUE

Milli rose from the bed, stirred from sleep by the optimistic feeling that something was about to begin. The pleasant feeling of anticipation in her gut was a given when she was with Karan, always promising something new and better on the horizon. But it reached a fever pitch inside her, knowing what the morning would bring.

The end of night kissed the start of day, the sky lightening as the sun considered rising. Everything moved, sluggishly through the Chandigarh heat as the tree frogs hummed a softly song that sounded like a coda. The tall grass swaying in the yard reminded her of a hand waving goodbye. The moon in the sky cast a benevolent light across the lawn. Everything was beautiful. And she was leaving it behind.

This was her last night in Chandigarh before the start of her greatest adventure, and she was standing on the threshold of a world she had never seen before. Karan had handed her two first-class tickets to see it and she wouldn't waste them. Everything was at her fingertips and she was ready to reach out and take it. Her mother was clean and sober for the first time in years, chasing sobriety as desperately as she used to chase a fix. Her home was no longer hers, but Rahull had repaired it so well that it looked like the home from her childhood. There would always be a glass of sweet tea and an open door waiting for her there but she was no longer trapped. She was free. And her life was waiting for her. And Chandigarh? Chandigarh was letting her go.

Actually, her life was sleeping in the bed, his hands reaching towards the spot she had vacated. More beautiful than the Chandigarh night, more promising than their trip to Paris was Karan, healing, well, and closer to whole than he had ever been. A smile slid across her face at the sight of him lying there, peaceful in his sleep. He looked younger, unweighted by the world, while dreams flickered behind his eyelids. She wondered what he dreamed about. Walking unaided on two feet? Flying without wings over the ocean, his hand in hers?

Soon enough, all their dreams would become a reality. This was just the first step in a dance they would do together for the rest of their lives. And if she had to carry him through these first few movements, she would. Her love for him was strong enough to support both of them. She had promised to be his support system. And she meant to uphold that promise.

Being with Karan was every pleasure she'd ever imagined. It was reading books in bed and staying up too late talking so that a pleasant haze of sleepiness wrapped around her the rest of the day, reminding her that soon enough she could slide back into bed next to the other half of her body. It was licking chocolate off her fingers from the French pastries Karan ordered especially for her and not caring that he got crumbs on the sheets. It was his voice singing low in her ear, reciting poetry or making some joke that had her falling onto the carpet laughing. It was the smell of his skin, the feel of his body pressed close to hers, it was a thousand kisses between where they had started and where they were now. It was building a home in another person's body. Milli came alive when Karan's hand touched hers.

A groan from the bed snapped Milli out of her reverie. Karan woke slowly, blinking in the light. His hands sought out Milli and when he did not find her in the bed, he turned to look at her standing silhouetted in the light from the window. An easy smile fell across his face, boy-like and totally charming. Milli felt herself begin to melt. Like a magnet her body was drawn towards his, and when he reached for her, she had no choice but to fall into his arms. As if there were any other choice she could make.

'What're you doing up at this hour, my love? And so far away?' he asked her, his voice hazy with sleep. He ran a hand through her hair and she leaned into the touch, feeling joy at the sensation of his skin on hers. He smelled of sleep, soap and linen. Clean, masculine, and lovely. Her Karan.

'I keep forgetting I've taken off work. Every once in a while, I think I'll need sleep to get through another shift, but even then, I still can't seem to settle down and close my eyes. Sleep just seems impossible on a night like this,' she confessed.

'You don't have to sleep,' he shrugged, 'you just have to let me hold you until morning.'

'I feel like it's noon already,' she said. He had a strong hand wrapped around her wrist in a loose grip. She played with his fingers, flexing them and tracing her fingertips across his knuckles. 'I can't believe we're really doing this.'

'Believe it,' he whispered in her ear.

'Honestly?' she asked, a faint smile playing on her face as she remembered some of their first conversations.

'Honestly,' he said, tucking her against his chest. He wiggled his mouth as her hair tickled his lips, before pressing a kiss to the crown of her head. 'Now get some sleep, or at least close your eyes. The flight to Paris isn't for hours yet.'

'Less time than you might think,' she replied.

'Spend every moment of it with me,' he whispered back.

'Always,' she promised, letting her eyes fall closed.

'Bon Voyage,' its rays told her, sweet as syrup through the cracks in the blinds. 'Au revoir! Goodbye!'

———•———

The Chandigarh airport existed in the same state of flux as it always did, security check to baggage claim and everything in between churning out tourists and processing locals at a breakneck speed. Blink and you miss it. Blink and you miss your flight.

And in their midst, an island in the middle of a hurricane, was Milli with Karan by her side. She knew the airport like the back of her hand. She'd been there enough times, of course, though always on the other side of the counter of the duty free. Gate F11, right outside the duty free where she had struggled for years to make ends meet. But now she was holding the key to an international flight to Paris, courtesy of Air France in her hands. Two tickets, first class.

It was Karan's idea – a little getaway to celebrate the strides they had made since their fateful meeting. 'Chandigarh Hospital isn't the most romantic of getaways,' Karan joked, 'so what do you think about the Eiffel Tower? If you're desperate for the smell of antiseptic and post-op, we can do a quick tour of Hospital St Louis. I've heard it's lovely.'

'No more hospitals than necessary,' she responded, a grin on her face, 'God knows we've seen enough. Can we go to Shakespeare and Co instead?'

'Whatever you desire, we'll do,' he responded, returning her sappy smile.

So here they were, in love and brave together, her hands around the handles of his wheelchair as she wheeled him past the moving walkway and the mass of people gathered on each one. Both her carry-on and his were slung across her shoulder. They weighed a little more than other people's might but most sane people read less books than they did. Still, it suited her fine. They had made extra room in each suitcase to carry more on their way home from Paris.

'My French is terrible,' she protested when he'd first told her the idea earlier about visiting France together.

'Mine is worse,' he replied. 'They pretend not to understand English but we'll do fine.'

'I don't have anything to wear. I've heard Parisian ladies are very fashionable. It's kind of their thing,' she fretted, picking at her cuticles in an effort to keep the smile from her face.

'Then you can borrow my clothes! I've been told the Parisian ladies find me very fashionable.' She swatted at him as he grinned, ducking away from her as she reached to tickle his ribs.

He laughed, 'are you done finding excuses not to say yes?'

'Yes,' she had breathed, flinging herself into his arms. 'Yes. Let's go to Paris.'

And now here they were, in the airport, grinning broadly at each other as she wheeled Karan into the subway cart they had all to themselves. She could have used the walkway between terminals, following the walking path she used to take to keep her body from going numb during her shifts at the duty-free, but decided against it. The airport had installed the subway system for the express purpose of carting the millions of people who flew through the Chandigarh airport to their terminals, so there was no sense in not using them. Especially since she was now a patron, not an employee. When the train started moving again, Karan let out a sigh.

'I was worried,' he confessed, 'not recently. A few weeks ago, I was in so much pain and it didn't feel like the PT was helping at all. I relied on you for everything and I thought … ' he bit his lip, 'I thought a lot of things. That I'd never leave my house again. That you'd grow tired of me and leave me. That I'd get sick again and not be able to recover and leave you before we even started.'

The words escaped from him in a rush that startled Milli.

'Hey,' she comforted him, rubbing small circles into his shoulder, 'hey, Karan.'

'But now we're here and you're beside me and this is our life together, and I couldn't be happier. I thought I'd never leave the house again and here you are with me. We haven't even taken off yet but Milli, I feel like my heart is soaring. We're free,' he whispered. 'You and I. We're free.'

'I can't believe it either,' she whispered. 'Before I met you I couldn't have imagined anything like this. I thought I'd be born and buried on the same patch of land. But with you I have future. I have hope. I have a home. And I have my love by my side through it all. I don't know what the future has in store for us, but Paris is a good first step, don't you think?'

'Yes,' he answered, 'I definitely think so.'

The train slid to a stop at their terminal. Milli leaned in close to his ear. 'Are you ready to fly?' she asked.

'With you?' he smiled, 'always.'

When the doors opened, she wheeled Karan forward quickly, picking up speed as they darted through the flow of people, both of them shrieking with laughter as Milli navigated through the terminal as fast as she could. As they passed by the women's bathroom, her friend Harman poked her head out from the bathroom to see what all the commotion was about. No doubt she was hoping for great gossip to share with Milli at their next shift together.

'Milli Bajwa, what kind of trouble are you getting into this time?' she hollered, her hand on her hip and her mop in her other hand. Her eyes widened as she noticed Karan, 'and is this that boy you were telling me about? You said he was handsome but I didn't believe you!'

'We'll talk later, Harman, I've got a flight to catch!' Milli called over her shoulder.

'How handsome am I?' Karan asked when he could finally catch his breath.

'I try not to lie to Harman,' Milli grinned.

'Aww, I'm blushing.' Karan tilted his head up and Milli couldn't help but kiss him, long and hard, in front of everyone.

'How's that for blushing?' she asked when she pulled away.

'Adequate,' he teased, settling back against his chair as she slid into the seat next to him and extracted both their current novels out of their respective carry-ons.

'We've got a few minutes before we have to board,' she said, handing him his book.

'Honestly, love,' he replied, 'I can barely focus. You're so beautiful and I love you so much. I'm having a hard time getting past it. I've imagined you under the Paris lights at night for a while now. I never thought I'd get to see it. Especially not so soon.'

'We haven't actually gotten to Paris yet,' she teased, 'what if the plane crashes into the ocean and I get eaten by a shark?'

'That would be a shame,' he said softly.

'I'll do my best to fight them off,' she promised. 'I read in a book once that punching them in the nose works, but as I don't make a habit of swimming in shark-infested waters, I haven't had the chance to try it out yet.'

'I'll make a note for our next trip. Scuba diving so Milli can punch a shark.'

'I think there are laws against that,' she pondered. 'You know,' she said after a long moment, 'I've never gone scuba diving. But there are a lot of things I've never done. Never sailed on a sailboat. Or a yacht. Or any kind of seafaring boat, actually. Never eaten panna cotta, never seen the Statue of Liberty...'

'Most of those things are tragedies for me at least,' he told her, 'but the Statue of Liberty is an overrated experience. There are many far more interesting things in New York.'

'I've never been to New York, either,' she shrugged. 'Honestly, there's so little I've done. This is my first time on a plane, so.'

'Internationally?' he asked, puzzled.

'No, any plane,' she responded. 'That was a surprise I was trying to keep but I got too excited.'

'Really? You've never flown before? But surely—has anyone really not been on a plane?'

'I haven't,' she ticked off on her fingers, 'and neither did my mother, my grandparents, any of my aunts, most of my classmates...'

'Point taken,' he shrugged.

'But I have flown before,' she said softly in his ear. Her words were meant for him alone. 'I feel like I fly every time we kiss.'

With that she kissed him again, feeling his smile against hers as he kissed her back. Oblivious to the world around them, they held each other close, smiling. They had each other and needed nothing else.

They were in love. They were together. And together, they were free.